Family, that slippery word, a star to every wandering bark, and everyone sailing under a different sky

1 3 5 7 9 10 8 6 4 2

Vintage
20 Vauxhall Bridge Road,
London SW1V 2SA

Vintage Classics is part of the Penguin Random House
group of companies whose addresses can be found at
global.penguinrandomhouse.com

Penguin
Random House
UK

A Spot of Bother first published in Great Britain by Jonathan Cape in 2006
First published by Vintage in 2007
The Red House first published in Great Britain by Jonathan Cape in 2012
First published by Vintage in 2013
The Pier Falls first published in Great Britain by Jonathan Cape in 2016
First published by Vintage in 2017

This short edition published by Vintage in 2019

penguin.co.uk/vintage

A CIP catalogue record for this book is available from the British Library

ISBN 9781784874063

Typeset in 10.5/14.5 pt FreightText Pro
by Jouve (UK), Milton Keynes
Printed and bound in Great Britain by Clays Ltd, Elcograf S.p.A.

Penguin Random House is committed to a sustainable future for our
business, our readers and our planet. This book is made from Forest
Stewardship Council® certified paper.

Family

MARK HADDON

VINTAGE MINIS

Contents

A Spot of Bother

1

GEORGE POURED MORTAR onto the square of hardboard and checked it for lumps with the blade of the trowel.

It was like the fear of flying.

He picked up a brick, mortared the underside, laid it and shifted it gently sideways so that it sat snug against the upright spirit level.

It had not bothered him in the beginning, those bumpy rides on prop planes to Palma and Lisbon. His main memories were of sweaty pre-packed cheese and that roar as the toilet bowl opened into the stratosphere. Then the plane back from Lyons in 1979 had to be de-iced three times. At first he had noticed only that everyone in the departure lounge was driving him to distraction (Katie practising handstands, Jean going to the duty-free shop after their gate number had been called, the young man opposite stroking his excessively long hair as if it were some kind of tame creature . . .). And when they boarded, something in the cloistered, chemical air of the cabin itself had made his chest feel tight. But only when they were taxiing to the runway did he realise that the plane was going to suffer some catastrophic mechanical failure mid-flight and that he was going to cartwheel earthwards for several minutes inside a large steel tube with 200 strangers who were crying and soiling themselves, then die in a tangerine fireball of twisted steel.

He remembered Katie saying, 'Mum, I think there's something wrong with Dad,' but she seemed to be calling faintly from a tiny disc of sunlight at the top of a very deep well into which he had fallen.

He stared doggedly at the seat-back in front of him, trying desperately to pretend that he was sitting in the living room at home. But every few minutes he would hear a sinister chime and see a little red light flashing in the bulkhead to his right, secretly informing the cabin crew that the pilot was wrestling with some fatal malfunction in the cockpit.

It was not that he could not speak, more that speaking was something which happened in another world of which he had only the vaguest memory.

At some point Jamie looked out of the window and said, 'I think the wing's coming off.' Jean hissed, 'For God's sake, grow up,' and George actually felt the rivets blowing and the fuselage dropping like a ton of hardcore.

For several weeks afterwards he was unable to see a plane overhead without feeling angry.

It was a natural reaction. Human beings were not meant to be sealed into tins and fired through the sky by fan-assisted rockets.

He laid a brick at the opposite corner then stretched a line between the tops of the two bricks to keep the course straight.

Of course he felt appalling. That was what anxiety did, persuaded you to get out of dangerous situations fast. Leopards, big spiders, strange men coming across the river with spears. If anything it was other people who had the problem, sitting there reading the *Daily Express* and sucking boiled sweets as if they were on a large bus.

But Jean liked sun. And driving to the south of France would wreck a holiday before it had begun. So he needed a strategy to prevent the horror taking hold in May and spiralling towards some kind of seizure at Heathrow in July. Squash, long walks, cinema, Tony Bennett at full volume, the first glass of red wine at six, a new *Flashman* novel.

He heard voices and looked up. Jean, Katie and

Ray were standing on the patio like dignitaries waiting for him to dock at some foreign quay.

'George . . . ?'

'Coming.' He removed the excess mortar from around the newly laid brick, scraped the remainder back into the bucket and replaced the lid. He stood up and walked down the lawn, cleaning his hands on a rag.

'Katie has some news,' said Jean, in the voice she used when she was ignoring the arthritis in her knee. 'But she didn't want to tell me until you were here.'

'Ray and I are getting married,' said Katie.

George had a brief out-of-body experience. He was looking down from fifteen feet above the patio, watching himself as he kissed Katie and shook Ray's hand. It was like falling off that stepladder. The way time slowed down. The way your body knew instinctively how to protect your head with your arms.

'I'll put some champagne into the freezer,' Jean said, trotting back into the house.

George re-entered his body.

'End of September,' said Ray. 'Thought we'd keep it simple. Not put you folks to too much trouble.'

'Right,' said George. 'Right.'

He would have to make a speech at the reception, a speech that said nice things about Ray. Jamie would refuse to come to the wedding. Jean would refuse to allow Jamie to refuse to come to the wedding. Ray was going to be a member of the family. They would see him all the time. Until they died. Or emigrated.

What was Katie doing? You could not control children, he knew that. Making them eat vegetables was hard enough. But marrying Ray? She had a 2:1 in Philosophy. And that chap who had climbed into her car in Leeds. She had given the police a part of his ear.

Jacob appeared in the doorway wielding a bread-knife. 'I'm an effelant and I'm going to catch the train and . . . and . . . and . . . and this is my tusks.'

Katie raised her eyebrows. 'I'm not sure that's an entirely good idea.'

Jacob ran back into the kitchen squealing with joy. Katie stepped into the doorway after him. 'Come here, Monkey Biscuits.'

And George was alone with Ray.

Ray's brother was in jail.

Ray worked for an engineering company which made high-spec camshaft milling machines. George had absolutely no idea what these were.

'Well.'

'Well.'

Ray crossed his arms. 'So, how's the studio going?'

'Hasn't fallen down yet.' George crossed his arms, realised that he was copying Ray and uncrossed them. 'Not that there's enough of it to fall down.'

They were silent for a very long time indeed. Ray rearranged three small pebbles on the flagstones with the toe of his right shoe. George's stomach made an audible noise.

Ray said, 'I know what you're thinking.'

For a short, horrified moment George thought Ray might be telling the truth.

'My being divorced and everything.' He pursed his lips and nodded slowly. 'I'm a lucky guy, George. I know that. I'll look after your daughter. You don't need to worry on that score.'

'Good,' said George.

'We'd like to foot the bill,' said Ray, 'unless you have any objections. I mean, you've already had to do it once.'

'No. You shouldn't have to pay,' said George, glad to be able to pull rank a little. 'Katie's our daughter. We should make sure she's sent off in style.' *Sent off?* It made Katie sound like a ship.

'Fair play to you,' said Ray.

It wasn't simply that Ray was working class, or that he spoke with a rather strong northern accent. George was not a snob, and whatever his background, Ray had certainly made good, judging by the size of his car and Katie's descriptions of their house.

The main problem, George felt, was Ray's size. He looked like an ordinary person who had been magnified. He moved more slowly than other people, the way the larger animals in zoos did. Giraffes. Buffalo. He lowered his head to go through doorways and had what Jamie unkindly but accurately described as *strangler's hands*.

During thirty-five years on the fringes of the manufacturing industry George had worked with manly men of all stripes. Big men, men who could open beer bottles with their teeth, men who had killed people during active military service, men who, in Ted Monk's charming phrase, would shag anything that stood still for long enough. And though he had never felt entirely at home in their company, he had rarely felt cowed. But when Ray visited, he was reminded of being with his older brother's friends when he was fourteen, the suspicion that there was a secret code of manhood to which he was not privy.

'Honeymoon?' asked George.

'Barcelona,' said Ray.

'Nice,' said George, who was briefly unable to remember which country Barcelona was in. 'Very nice.'

'Hope so,' said Ray. 'Should be a bit cooler that time of year.'

George asked how Ray's work was going and Ray said they'd taken over a firm in Cardiff which made horizontal machining centres.

And it was all right. George could do the bluff repartee about cars and sport if pressed. But it was like being a sheep in the nativity play. No amount of applause was going to make the job seem dignified or stop him wanting to run home to a book about fossils.

'They've got big clients in Germany. The company were trying to get me to shuttle back and forth to Munich. Knocked that one on the head. For obvious reasons.'

The first time Katie had brought him home, Ray had run his finger along the rack of CDs above the television and said, 'So you're a jazz fan, Mr Hall,' and George had felt as if Ray had unearthed a stack of pornographic magazines.

Jean appeared at the door. 'Are you going to get cleaned and changed before lunch?'

George turned to Ray. 'I'll catch you later.' And he was away, through the kitchen, up the stairs and into the tiled quiet of the lockable bathroom.

2

THEY HATED THE idea. As predicted. Katie could tell.

Well, they could live with it. Time was she'd have gone off the deep end. In fact, there was a part of her which missed being the person who went off the deep end. Like her standards were slipping. But you reached a stage where you realised it was a waste of energy trying to change your parents' minds about anything, ever.

Ray wasn't an intellectual. He wasn't the most beautiful man she'd ever met. But the most beautiful man she'd ever met had shat on her from a great height. And when Ray put his arms around her she felt safer than she'd felt for a long time.

She remembered the grim lunch at Lucy's. The toxic goulash Barry had made. His drunken friend groping her arse in the kitchen and Lucy having that asthma attack. Looking out the window and seeing Ray with Jacob on his shoulders, playing horses, running round the lawn, jumping over the upturned wheelbarrow. And weeping at the thought of going back to their tiny flat with the dead animal smell.

Then he turned up at her door with a bunch of carnations, which freaked her out a bit. He didn't want to come in. But she insisted. Out of embarrassment, mostly. Not wanting to take the flowers and shut the door in his face. She made him a coffee and he said he wasn't good at chatting and she asked if he wanted to skip straight to the sex. But it sounded funnier inside her head than out. And in truth, if he'd said, 'OK', she might have accepted just because it was flattering to be wanted, in spite of the bags under her eyes and the Cotswold Wildlife Park T-shirt with the banana stains. But he meant it, about the chatting. He was good at mending the cassette player and cooking fried breakfasts and organising expeditions to railway museums, and he preferred all of them to small talk.

He had a temper. He'd put his hand through a door towards the end of his first marriage and severed two tendons in his wrist. But he was one of the gentlest men she knew.

A month later he took them up to Hartlepool to visit his father and stepmother. They lived in a bungalow with a garden which Jacob thought was heaven on account of the three gnomes around the ornamental pond and the gazebo thing you could hide in.

Alan and Barbara treated her like the squire's daughter, which was unnerving till she realised they probably treated all strangers the same way. Alan had worked in a sweet factory for most of his life. When Ray's mother died of cancer, he started going to the church he'd gone to as a boy and met Barbara who'd divorced her husband when he became an alcoholic (*took to drink*, was the phrase she used, which made it sound like morris dancing or hedge-laying).

They seemed more like grandparents to Katie (though neither of her own grandfathers had tattoos). They belonged to an older world of deference and duty. They'd covered the wall of their living room with photos of Ray and Martin, the same number of each despite the unholy mess Martin had made of his life. There was a small cabinet of china figurines in the dining room and a fluffy U-shaped carpet around the base of the loo.

Barbara cooked a stew, then grilled some fish fingers for Jacob when he complained about the 'lumpy bits'. They asked what she did in London and she explained how she helped run an arts festival, and it sounded fey and crapulous. So she told the story of the drunken newsreader they'd booked the previous year, and remembered, just a little bit too late, the reason for Barbara's divorce and didn't even manage a graceful change of subject, just ground to an embarrassed halt. So Barbara changed the subject by asking what her parents did and Katie said Dad had recently retired from managing a small company. She was going to leave it there but Jacob said, 'Grandpa makes swings,' so she had to explain that Shepherds built equipment for children's playgrounds, which sounded better than running an arts festival, though not quite as solid as she wished.

And maybe a couple of years ago she'd have felt uncomfortable and wanted to get back to London as fast as possible, but many of her childless London friends were beginning to seem a little fey and crapulous themselves, and it was good to spend time with people who'd brought up children of their own, and listened more than they talked, and thought gardening was more important than getting your hair cut.

And maybe they were old-fashioned. Maybe Ray was old-fashioned. Maybe he didn't like hoovering. Maybe he always put the tampon box back into the bathroom cupboard. But Graham did t'ai chi and turned out to be a wanker.

She didn't give a toss what her parents thought. Besides, Mum was shagging one of Dad's old colleagues, and Dad was pretending the silk scarves and the twinkle were all down to her new job at the bookshop. So they weren't in a position to lecture anyone when it came to relationships.

Jesus, she didn't even want to think about it.

3

JAMIE ATE A seventh Pringle, put the tube back in the cupboard, went into the living room, slumped onto the sofa and pressed the button on the answerphone.

'Jamie. Hello. It's Mum. I thought I might catch you in. Oh well, never mind. I'm sure you've heard the news already, but Katie and Ray were round on Sunday and they're getting married. Which was a bit of a surprise, as you can imagine. Your father's still recovering. Anyway. Third weekend in September. We're having the reception here. In the garden. Katie said you should bring someone. But we'll be sending out proper invitations nearer the time. Anyway, it would be lovely to talk to you when you get the chance. Lots of love.'

Married? Jamie felt a little wobbly. He replayed the message in case he'd heard it wrong. He hadn't.

God, his sister had done some stupid things in her time but this took the biscuit. Ray was meant to be a stage. Katie spoke French. Ray read biographies of sports personalities. Buy him a few pints and he'd probably start sounding off about *our coloured brethren*.

They'd been living together for what . . . ? Six months?

He listened to the message for a third time, then went into the kitchen and got a choc-ice from the freezer.

It shouldn't have pissed him off. He hardly saw Katie these days. And when he did she had Ray in tow. What difference did it make if they were married? A bit of paper, that was all.

So why did he feel churned up about it?

There was a bloody cat in the garden. He picked up a piece of gravel from the step, took aim and missed.

Fuck. There was ice cream on his shirt from the recoil.

He dabbed it off with a wet sponge.

Hearing the news second-hand. That's what pissed him off. Katie hadn't dared tell him. She knew what he'd say. Or what he'd think. So she'd given the job to Mum.

It was the other people thing in a nutshell. Coming along and fucking things up. You were driving through Streatham minding your own business and they ploughed into your passenger door while talking on their mobile. You went away to Edinburgh for a long weekend and they nicked your laptop and shat on the sofa.

He looked outside. The bloody cat was back. He put the choc-ice down and threw another piece of gravel, harder this time. It glanced off one of the sleepers, flew over the end wall into the adjoining garden and hit some invisible object with a loud *crack*.

He shut the French windows, picked up the choc-ice and stepped out of sight.

Two years ago Katie wouldn't have given Ray the time of day.

She was exhausted. That was the problem. She wasn't thinking straight. Looking after Jacob on six hours sleep a night in that craphole of a flat for two years. Then Ray pitches up with the money and the big house and the flash car.

He had to call her. He put the choc-ice on the window sill.

Perhaps it was Ray who'd told their parents. That was a definite possibility. And very Ray. Marching in with his size fourteen boots. Then getting shit from Katie on the way home for stealing her thunder.

He dialled. The phone rang at the far end.

The phone was picked up, Jamie realised it might be Ray and very nearly dropped the receiver. 'Shit.'

'Hello?' It was Katie.

'Thank God,' said Jamie. 'Sorry. I didn't mean that. I mean, it's Jamie.'

'Jamie, hi.'

'Mum just told me the news.' He tried to sound

breezy and unconcerned, but he was still jumpy on account of the Ray panic.

'Yeh, we only decided to announce it on the way to Peterborough. Then we got back and Jacob was being rather high-maintenance. I was going to ring you tonight.'

'So . . . congratulations.'

'Thanks,' said Katie.

Then there was an uncomfortable pause. He wanted Katie to say, *Help me, Jamie, I'm making a terrible mistake*, which she obviously wasn't going to do. And he wanted to say, *What the fuck are you doing?* But if he did that she'd never speak to him again.

He asked how Jacob was doing and Katie talked about him drawing a rhinoceros at nursery and doing a poo in the bath, so he changed the subject and said, 'Tony's getting an invite, then?'

'Of course.'

And it suddenly sank in. The joint invitation. No bloody way was he taking Tony to Peterborough.

After putting the phone down he picked up the choc-ice, wiped the brown dribble off the window sill and walked back into the kitchen to make some tea.

Tony in Peterborough. Jesus. He wasn't sure which was worse. Mum and Dad pretending Tony was one of Jamie's colleagues in case the neighbours found out. Or their being painfully groovy about it.

The most likely combination, of course, was Mum

being painfully groovy and Dad pretending Tony was one of Jamie's colleagues. And Mum being angry with Dad for pretending Tony was one of Jamie's colleagues. And Dad being angry with Mum for being painfully groovy.

He didn't even want to think about Ray's friends. He'd known enough Rays in college. Eight pints and they were that close to lynching the nearest homosexual for sport. Apart from the closet case. There was always a closet case. And sooner or later they got paralytic and sidled up to you in the bar and told you everything, then got shirty when you wouldn't take them up to your room and give them a handjob.

He wondered what Jeff Weller was doing these days. A sexless marriage in Saffron Walden, probably, with some back copies of *Zipper* hidden behind the hot water tank.

Jamie had spent a great deal of time and energy arranging his life precisely as he wanted. Work. Home. Family. Friends. Tony. Exercise. Relaxation. Some compartments you could mix. Katie and Tony. Friends and exercise. But the compartments were there for a reason. It was like a zoo. You could mix chimpanzees and parrots. But take the cages away altogether and you had a bloodbath on your hands.

He wouldn't tell Tony about the invitation. That was the answer. It was simple.

He looked down at the stub of choc-ice. What

was he doing? He'd bought them to console himself after the binoculars argument. He should have chucked them the next day.

He pushed the choc-ice into the bin, retrieved the other four from the freezer and shoved them in afterwards.

He stuck *Born to Run* on the CD player and made a pot of tea. He washed up and cleaned the draining board. He poured a mug of tea, added some semi-skimmed milk and wrote a cheque for the gas bill.

Bruce Springsteen was sounding particularly smug this evening. Jamie ejected him and read the *Telegraph*.

Just after eight, Tony turned up in a jovial mood, loped into the hall, bit the back of Jamie's neck, threw himself lengthways on the sofa and began rolling a cigarette.

Jamie wondered, sometimes, if Tony had been a dog in a previous life and not quite made the transition properly. The appetite. The energy. The lack of social graces. The obsession with smells (Tony would put his nose into Jamie's hair and inhale and say, 'Ooh, where have you been?').

Jamie slid an ashtray down to Tony's end of the coffee table and sat down. He lifted Tony's legs into his lap and began unlacing his boots.

He wanted to strangle Tony sometimes. The poor house-training mostly. Then he'd catch sight of him across a room and see those long legs and that brawny, farmboy amble and feel exactly what he felt that first time. Something in the pit of his stomach, almost painful, the need to be held by this man. And no one else made him feel like that.

'Nice day at the office?' asked Tony.

'It was, actually.'

'So why the Mr Glum vibes?'

'What Mr Glum vibes?' asked Jamie.

'The fish mouth, the crinkly forehead.'

Jamie slumped backwards into the sofa and closed his eyes. 'You remember Ray . . .'

'Ray . . . ?'

'Katie's boyfriend, Ray.'

'Yu-huh.'

'She's marrying him.'

'OK.' Tony lit his cigarette. A little strand of burning tobacco fell onto his jeans and went out. 'We bundle her into a car and take her to a safe house somewhere in Gloucestershire . . .'

'Tony . . .' said Jamie.

'What?'

'Let's try it again, all right?'

Tony held his hands up in mock-surrender. 'Sorry.'

'Katie is marrying Ray,' said Jamie.

'Which is not good.'

'No.'

'So you're going to try and stop her,' said Tony.

'She's not in love with him,' said Jamie. 'She just

wants someone with a steady job and a big house who can help look after Jacob.'

'There are worse reasons for marrying someone.'

'You'd hate him,' said Jamie.

'So?' asked Tony.

'She's my sister.'

'And you're going to . . . what?' asked Tony.

'God knows.'

'This is her life, Jamie. You can't fight off Anne Bancroft with a crucifix and drag her onto the nearest bus.'

'I'm not trying to stop her.' Jamie was starting to regret this topic of conversation. Tony didn't know Katie. He'd never met Ray. In truth, Jamie just wanted him to say, *You're absolutely right*. But Tony had never said that, to anyone, about anything. Not even when drunk. Especially not when drunk. 'It's her business. Obviously. It's just . . .'

'She's an adult,' said Tony. 'She has the right to screw things up.'

Neither of them said anything for a few moments.

'So, am I invited?' Tony blew a little plume of smoke towards the ceiling.

Jamie paused a fraction of a second too long before answering, and Tony did that suspicious thing with his eyebrows. So Jamie had to change tactics on the hoof. 'I'm sincerely hoping it's not going to happen.'

'But if it does?'

There was no point fighting over this. Not now.

When Jehovah's Witnesses knocked on the door Tony invited them in for tea. Jamie took a deep breath. 'Mum did mention bringing someone.'

'Someone?' said Tony. 'Charming.'

'You don't actually want to come, do you?'

'Why not?' asked Tony.

'Ray's engineering colleagues, my mother fussing over you . . .'

'You're not listening to what I'm saying, are you?' Tony took hold of Jamie's chin and squished it, the way aunts did when you were a kid. 'I would like. To come. To your sister's wedding. With you.'

A police car tore past the end of the cul-de-sac with its siren going. Tony was still holding Jamie's chin. Jamie said, 'Let's talk about it later, OK?'

Tony tightened his grip, pulled Jamie towards him and sniffed. 'What have you been eating?'

'Choc-ice.'

'God. This thing really has depressed you, hasn't it?'

'I threw the rest away,' said Jamie.

Tony stubbed out his cigarette. 'Go and get me one. I haven't had a choc-ice since . . . God, Brighton in about 1987.'

Jamie went into the kitchen, retrieved one of the choc-ices from the bin, rinsed the ketchup from the wrapper and took it back through to the living room.

If his luck was in, Katie would throw a toaster at Ray before September and there wouldn't be a wedding.

4

JEAN UNDRESSED WHILE David was showering and slipped into the dressing gown he'd left out for her. She wandered over to the bay window and sat on the arm of the chair.

It made her feel attractive. Just being in this room. The cream walls. The wooden floor. The big fish print in the metal frame. It was like one of those rooms you saw in magazines which made you think about living a different life.

She gazed onto the oval lawn. Three shrubs in big stone pots on one side. Three on the other. A folding wooden lounger.

She enjoyed making love, but she enjoyed this too. The way she could think here, without the rest of her life rushing in and crowding her.

Jean rarely spoke about her parents. People simply didn't understand. They were teenagers before it dawned on them that Auntie Mary from next door was their father's girlfriend. Everyone pictured some kind of steamy soap opera. But there was no intrigue, no blazing rows. Her father worked in the same bank for forty years and made wooden birdhouses in the cellar. And whatever her mother felt about their bizarre domestic arrangement she never spoke about it, even after Jean's father died.

Her guess was that she never spoke about it when he was alive either. It happened. Appearances were kept up. End of story.

Jean felt ashamed. As any sane person would. If you kept quiet about it you felt like a liar. If you told the story you felt like something from a circus.

No wonder the children all headed off so fast in such different directions. Eileen to her religion. Douglas to his articulated lorries. And Jean to George.

They met at Betty's wedding.

There was something formal about him, almost military. Handsome in a way that young men no longer were these days.

Everyone was being rather silly (Betty's brother, the one who died in that horrible factory accident, had made a hat out of a napkin and was singing 'I've got a lovely bunch of coconuts' to much general hilarity). Jean could see that George was finding it all rather tiresome. She wanted to tell him that she was finding it all rather tiresome, too, but he didn't look like someone you could talk to, like that, out of the blue.

Ten minutes later he was at her side, offering to get her another drink, and she made a fool of herself by asking for a lemonade, to show that she was sober and sensible, then asking for wine because she didn't want to seem childish, then changing her mind a second time because he really was very attractive and she was getting a bit flustered.

He invited her out for dinner the following week and she didn't want to go. She knew what would happen. He was honest and utterly dependable and she was going to fall in love with him, and when he found out about her family he was going to disappear in a cloud of smoke. Like Roger Hamilton. Like Pat Lloyd.

Then he told her about his father drinking himself into a stupor and sleeping face down on the lawn. And his mother crying in the bathroom. And his uncle going mad and ending up in some dreadful hospital. At which point she just took hold of his face and kissed him, which was something she'd never done to a man before.

And it wasn't that he'd changed over the years. He was still honest. He was still dependable. But the world had changed. And so had she.

If anything it was those French cassettes (were they a present from Katie? she really couldn't remember). They were going to the Dordogne, and she had time on her hands.

A few months later she was standing in a shop in

Bergerac buying bread and cheese and these little spinach tarts and the woman was apologising for the weather and Jean found herself striking up an actual conversation while George sat on a bench across the street counting his mosquito bites. And nothing happened there and then, but when she got home it seemed a bit cold, a bit small, a bit English.

Through the wall she heard the faint sound of the shower door popping open.

That it should be David, of all people, amazed her still. She'd cooked him spaghetti bolognese on one occasion. She'd made small talk about the new conservatory and come away feeling dull but thankfully invisible. He wore linen jackets and rollneck sweaters in peach and sky blue and smoked little cigars. He'd lived in Stockholm for three years and when he and Mina separated amicably it only increased the sense that he was a little too modern for Peterborough.

He retired early, George lost touch with him and he didn't cross her mind until she looked up from her till in Ottakar's one day and saw him holding a copy of *The Naked Chef* and a tin of Maisie Mouse pencils.

They had a coffee across the street and when she talked about going to Paris with Ursula he didn't mock her, like Bob Green used to do. Or wonder how two middle-aged ladies could survive a long weekend in a foreign city without being mugged or strangled or sold into the white slave trade, like George had done.

And it wasn't that she was physically attracted to him (he was shorter than her and there was quite a lot of black hair protruding from his cuffs). But she never met men over fifty who were still interested in the world around them, in new people, new books, new countries.

It was like talking to a female friend. Except that he was a man. And they'd only known each other for about fifteen minutes. Which was very disconcerting.

The following week they were standing on a foot-bridge over the dual carriageway and that feeling welled up inside her. The one she got by the sea some-times. Ships disembarking, gulls squabbling over the wake, those mournful horns. The realisation that you could sail off into the blue and start again in a new place.

He took her hand and held it, and she was disap-pointed. She'd found a soulmate and he was about to wreck it all with a clumsy pass. But he squeezed it and let go and said, 'Come on. You'll be late home,' and she wanted to take his hand back.

Later she was scared. Of saying yes. Of saying no. Of saying yes then realising she should have said no. Of saying no then realising she should have said yes. Of being naked in front of another man when her body sometimes made her feel like weeping.

So she told George. About meeting David in the shop and the coffee across the road. But not about the hands and the footbridge. She wanted him to be cross. She wanted him to make her life simple again. But he didn't. She dropped David's name into the conversation a couple more times and got no reaction. George's lack of concern began to seem like encouragement.

David had had other affairs. She knew. Even before he said. The way he cupped his hand round the back of her neck that first time. She was relieved. She didn't want to do this with someone sailing into uncharted waters, especially after Gloria's horror story about finding that man from Derby parked outside her house one morning.

And Jean was right. He was very hairy indeed. Like a monkey, almost. Which made it better somehow. Because it showed that it wasn't really about the sex. Though, during the last few months she had grown rather fond of that silky feel under her fingers when she stroked his back.

The bathroom door clicked open and she closed her eyes. David walked across the rug and slipped his arms around her. She could smell coal tar soap and clean skin. She could feel his breath on the back of her neck.

He said, 'I seem to have found a beautiful woman in my bedroom.'

She laughed at the childishness of it. She was very far from being a beautiful woman. But it was good, pretending. Almost better than the real thing. Like being a kid again. Getting this close to another human being. Climbing trees and drinking bathwater. Knowing how everything felt and tasted.

He turned her round and kissed her.

He wanted to make her feel good. She couldn't remember the last time someone had done that.

He closed the curtains and led her over to the bed and laid her down and kissed her again and pushed the dressing gown off her shoulders and she was melting into that dark behind her eyelids, the way butter melted in a hot pan, the way you melted back into sleep after waking up at night, just letting it take you.

She put her hands around his neck and felt the muscles under the skin and those tiny hairs where the barber had run the razor close. And his own hands were slowly moving down her body and she could see the two of them from the far side of the room, doing this thing you only ever saw beautiful people doing in films. And maybe she did believe it now, that she was beautiful, that they were both beautiful.

Her body felt as if it were swaying back and forth with the movement of his fingers, a fairground ride that was taking her higher and faster with each swing so that she was weightless at each end, so high she could see the pleasure gardens and the ferries in the bay and the green hills across the water.

He said, 'God, I love you,' and she loved him back, for doing this, for understanding a part of her that she never knew existed. But she couldn't say it. Not now. She couldn't say anything. She just squeezed his shoulder, meaning, *Keep going*.

She put her hand around his penis and moved it back and forth and it no longer seemed strange, not even a part of his body, more a part of hers, the sensations flowing in one unbroken circle. And she could hear herself panting now, like a dog, but she didn't care.

And she realised that it was going to happen and she heard herself saying, 'Yes, yes, yes,' and even hearing the sound of her own voice didn't break the spell. And it swept over her like surf sweeping over sand then falling back and sweeping up over the sand again and falling back.

Images went off in her head like little fireworks. The smell of coconut. Brass firedogs. The starched bolster in her parents' bed. A hot cone of grass-clippings. She was breaking up into a thousand tiny pieces, like snow, or bonfire sparks, tumbling high in the air, then starting to fall, so slowly it hardly seemed like falling at all.

She held his wrist to stop his hand and lay there with her eyes closed, dizzy and out of breath.

She was crying.

It was like finding your body again after fifty years and realising you were old friends and suddenly understanding why you'd felt so alone all this time.

She opened her eyes. David was looking down at her and she knew that she didn't need to explain anything.

He waited for a couple of minutes. 'And now,' he said, 'I think it's my turn.'

He got to his knees and moved between her legs. He opened her gently with his fingers and pushed himself inside. And this time she watched him as he rolled forwards onto his arms until she was full of him.

Sometimes she enjoyed the fact that he was doing this to her. Sometimes she enjoyed the fact that she was doing this to him. Today the distinction didn't seem to exist.

He began to move faster and his eyes narrowed with pleasure and finally closed. So she closed her own eyes and held onto his arms and let herself be rocked back and forth, and finally he reached a climax and held himself inside her and did that little animal shiver. And when he opened his eyes he was breathing heavily and smiling.

She smiled back at him.

Katie was right. You spent your life giving everything to other people, so they could drift away, to school, to college, to the office, to Hornsey, to Ealing. So little of the love came back.

She had earned this. She deserved to feel like someone in a film.

He lowered himself gently to her side and pulled her head onto his shoulder so that she could see tiny beads of sweat in a line down the centre of his chest and hear his heart beating.

She closed her eyes again, and in the darkness she could feel the whole world revolving.

5

IT BLEW UP on Saturday morning.

Tony woke early and headed to the kitchen to make breakfast. When Jamie ambled down twenty minutes later Tony was sitting at the table emanating bad vibes.

Jamie had clearly done something wrong. 'What's up?'

Tony chewed his cheek and drummed the table with a teaspoon. 'This wedding,' said Tony.

'Look,' said Jamie. 'I don't particularly want to go myself.' He glanced at the clock. Tony had to leave in twenty minutes. Jamie realised that he should have stayed in bed.

'But you're going to go,' said Tony.

'I don't really have much choice.'

'So, why don't you want me to come with you?'

'Because you'll have a shit time,' said Jamie, 'and I'll have a shit time. And it doesn't matter that I'm having a shit time because they're my family, for better or worse. So every now and then I have to grit my teeth and put up with having a shit time for the greater good. But I'd rather not be responsible for you having a shit time on top of everything else.'

'It's only a fucking wedding,' said Tony. 'It's not transatlantic yachting. How shit can it be?'

'It's not just a fucking wedding,' said Jamie. 'It's my sister marrying the wrong person. For the second time in her life. Except this time we know it in advance. It's hardly a cause for celebration.'

'I don't give a fuck who she's marrying,' said Tony.

'Well, I do,' said Jamie.

'Who she's marrying is not the point,' said Tony.

Jamie called Tony an unsympathetic shit. Tony called Jamie a self-centred cunt. Jamie refused to discuss the subject any further. Tony stormed out.

Jamie smoked three cigarettes and fried himself two slices of eggy bread and realised he wasn't going to get anything constructive done so he might as well drive up to Peterborough and hear the wedding story first hand from Mum and Dad.

6

GEORGE WAS FITTING the window frames. There were six courses above the sill on either side. Enough brickwork to hold them firm. He spread the mortar and slotted the first one into place.

In truth it wasn't just the flying. Holidays themselves were not much further up George's list of favourite occupations. Visiting amphitheatres, walking the Pembrokeshire coast path, learning to ski. He could see the rationale behind these activities. One grim fortnight in Sicily had been made almost worthwhile by the mosaics at Piazza Armerina. What he failed to comprehend was packing oneself off to a foreign country to lounge by pools and eat plain food and cheap wine made somehow glorious by a view of a fountain and a waiter with a poor command of English.

They knew what they were doing in the Middle Ages. Holy days. Pilgrimages. Canterbury and Santiago de Compostela. Twenty hard miles a day, simple inns and something to aim for.

Norway might have been OK. Mountains, tundra, rugged shorelines. But it had to be Rhodes or Corsica. And in summer to boot, so that freckled Englishmen had to sit under awnings reading last week's *Sunday Times* while the sweat ran down their backs.

Now that he thought about it, he had been suffering from heatstroke during the visit to Piazza Armerina and most of what he recalled about the mosaics was from the stack of postcards he'd bought in the shop before retiring to the hire car with a bottle of water and a pack of Nurofen.

The human mind was not designed for sunbathing and light novels. Not on consecutive days at any rate. The human mind was designed for doing stuff. Making spears, hunting antelope . . .

The Dordogne in 1984 was the nadir. Diarrhoea, moths like flying hamsters, the blowtorch heat. Awake at three in the morning on a damp and lumpy mattress. Then the storm. Like someone hammering sheets of tin. Lightning so bright it came through the pillow. In the morning sixty, seventy dead frogs turning slowly in the pool. And at the far end something larger and furrier, a cat perhaps, or the Franzettis' dog, which Katie was poking with a snorkel.

He needed a drink. He walked back across the lawn and was removing his dirty boots when he saw

Jamie in the kitchen, dumping his bag and putting the kettle on.

He stopped and watched, the way he might stop and watch if there was a deer in the garden, which there was occasionally.

Jamie was a bit of a secretive creature himself. Not that he hid things. But he was reserved. Rather old-fashioned, now that George came to think about it. Different clothes and hairstyle and you could see him lighting a cigarette in a Berlin alleyway, or obscured by steam on a station platform.

Unlike Katie, who didn't know the meaning of the word *reserve*. The only person he knew who could bring up the subject of menstruation over lunch. And you still knew she was hiding things, things that were going to be dropped on you at random intervals. Like the wedding. Next week she would doubtless announce that she was pregnant.

Dear God. The wedding. Jamie must have come about the wedding.

He could do it. If Jamie wanted a double bed he would say the spare room was being used by someone else, and book him into an upmarket bed-and-breakfast somewhere. Just so long as George didn't have to use the word *boyfriend*.

He came round from his reverie and realised that Jamie was waving from inside the kitchen and looking a little troubled by George's lack of response.

He waved back, removed his other boot and went inside.

'What brings you to this neck of the woods?'

'Oh, just popping in,' said Jamie.

'Your mother didn't mention anything.'

'I didn't ring.'

'Never mind. I'm sure she can stretch lunch to three.'

'It's OK. I wasn't planning on staying. Tea?' asked Jamie.

'Thank you.' George got the digestives out while Jamie put a bag into a second mug.

'So. This wedding,' said Jamie.

'What about it?' asked George, trying to sound as if the subject had not yet occurred to him.

'What do you think?'

'I think . . .' George sat down and adjusted the chair so that it was precisely the right distance from the table. 'I think you should bring someone.'

There. That sounded pretty neutral as far as he could tell.

'No, Dad,' said Jamie wearily. 'I mean Katie and Ray. What do you think about them getting married?'

It was true. There really was no limit to the ways in which you could say the wrong thing to your children. You offered an olive branch and it was the wrong olive branch at the wrong time.

'Well?' Jamie asked again.

'To be honest, I'm trying to maintain a Buddhist detachment about the whole thing to stop it taking ten years off my life.'

'But she's serious, yeh?'

'Your sister is serious about everything. Whether she'll be serious about it in a fortnight's time is anyone's guess.'

'But what did she say?'

'Just that they were getting married. Your mother can fill you in on the emotional side of things. I'm afraid I was stuck talking to Ray.'

Jamie put a mug of tea down in front of George and raised his eyebrows. 'Bet that was a white-knuckle thrill ride.'

And there it was, that little door, opening briefly.

They had never done the father-son stuff. A couple of Saturday afternoons at Silverstone race track. Putting up the garden shed together. That was about it.

On the other hand, he saw friends doing the father-son stuff and as far as he could see it amounted to little more than sitting in adjacent seats at rugby matches and sharing vulgar jokes. Mothers and daughters, that made sense. Dresses. Gossip. All in all, not doing the father-son stuff probably counted as a lucky escape.

Yet there were moments like this when he saw how alike he and Jamie were.

'Ray is, I confess, rather hard work,' said George.

'In my long and sorry experience' – he dunked a biscuit – 'trying to change your sister's mind is a pointless exercise. I guess the gameplan is to treat her like an adult. Keep a stiff upper lip. Be nice to Ray. If it all goes pear-shaped in two years' time, well, we've had some practice in that department. The last thing I want to do is to let your sister know that we disapprove, then have Ray as a disgruntled son-in-law for the next thirty years.'

Jamie drank his tea. 'I'm just . . .'

'What?'

'Nothing. You're probably right. We should let her get on with it.'

Jean appeared in the doorway bearing a basket of dirty clothes. 'Hello, Jamie. This is a nice surprise.'

'Hi, Mum.'

'Well, here's your second opinion,' said George.

Jean put the basket on the washing machine. 'About what?'

'Jamie was wondering whether we should save Katie from a reckless and inadvisable marriage.'

'Dad . . .' said Jamie tetchily.

And this was where Jamie and George parted company. Jamie couldn't really do jokes, not at his own expense. He was, to be honest, a little delicate.

'George.' Jean glared at him accusingly. 'What have you been saying?'

George refused to rise to the bait.

'I'm just worried about Katie,' said Jamie.

'We're all worried about Katie,' said Jean, starting to fill the washing machine. 'Ray wouldn't be my first choice, either. But there you go. Your sister's a woman who knows her own mind.'

Jamie stood up. 'I'd better be going.'

Jean stopped filling the washing machine. 'You've only just got here.'

'I know. I should have phoned, really. I just wanted to know what Katie had said. I'd better be heading off.'

And he was gone.

Jean turned to George. 'Why do you always have to rub him up the wrong way?'

George bit his tongue. Again.

'Jamie?' Jean headed into the hallway.

George recalled only too well how much he had hated his own father. A friendly ogre who found coins in your ear and made origami squirrels and who shrank slowly over the years into an angry, drunken little man who thought praising children made them weak and never admitted that his own brother was schizophrenic, and who kept on shrinking so that by the time George and Judy and Brian were old enough to hold him to account he had performed the most impressive trick of all by turning into a self-pitying arthritic figure too insubstantial to be the butt of any-one's anger.

Perhaps the best you could hope for was not to do the same thing to your own children.

Jamie was a good lad. Not the most robust of chaps. But they got on well enough.

Jean returned to the kitchen. 'He's gone. What was that all about?'

'Lord alone knows.' George stood up and dropped his empty mug into the sink. 'The mystery of one's children is never-ending.'

7

JAMIE PULLED INTO a lay-by at the edge of the village.

I think you should bring someone.

Christ. You avoided the subject for twenty years then it flashed past at eighty and vanished in a cloud of exhaust.

Had he been wrong about his father all along? Was it possible that he could've come out at sixteen and got no shit whatsoever? *Totally understand. Chap at school. Keen on other chaps. Ended up playing cricket for Leicestershire.*

Jamie was angry. Though it was hard to put a finger on precisely who he was angry with. Or why.

It was the same feeling he got every time he visited Peterborough. Every time he saw photographs of himself as a child. Every time he smelled plasticine or tasted fish fingers. He was nine again. Or twelve. Or fifteen. And it wasn't about his feelings for Ivan Dunne. Or his lack of feelings for Pan's People. It was the sickening realisation that he'd landed on the wrong planet. Or in the wrong family. Or in the wrong body. The realisation that he had no choice but to bide his time until he could get away and build a little world of his own in which he felt safe.

It was Katie who pulled him through. Telling him to ignore Greg Pattershall's gang. Saying graffiti only counted if it was spelled correctly. And she was right. They really did end up leading shitty little lives injecting heroin on some estate in Walton.

He was probably the only boy at school who'd learned self-defence from his sister. He'd tried it once, on Mark Rice, who slumped into a bush and bled horribly, scaring Jamie so much he never hit anyone again.

Now he'd lost his sister. And no one understood. Not even Katie.

He wanted to sit in her kitchen and pull faces for Jacob and drink tea and eat too much Marks & Spencer's date-and-walnut cake and . . . not even talk. Not even need to talk.

Fuck it. If he said the word *home* he was going to cry.

Maybe if he'd been better at staying in touch. Maybe if he'd eaten a little more date-and-walnut cake. If he'd invited her and Jacob over more often. If he'd lent her money . . .

This was pointless.

He turned the ignition on, pulled out of the lay-by and was nearly killed by a green Transit van.

8

KATIE HAD HAD a shitty week.

The festival programmes arrived on Monday and Patsy, who still couldn't spell *programme*, shocked everyone by knowing a fact, that the photo of Terry Jones on page seven was actually a photo of Terry Gilliam. Aidan bawled Katie out because admitting he'd cocked up wasn't one of the skills he'd learned on his MBA. She resigned. He refused to accept her resignation. And Patsy cried because people were shouting.

She left early to pick up Jacob from nursery and Jackie said he'd bitten two other children. She took him to one side and gave him a lecture about being like the meanie crocodile in *A Kiss Like This*. But Jacob wasn't doing recriminations that day. So she cut her losses and drove him home where she withheld his yoghurt until they'd had a conversation about biting, which generated the same kind of frustration

Dr Benson probably felt when they were doing Kant at university.

'It was my tractor,' said Jacob.

'Actually it's everyone's tractor,' said Katie.

'I was playing with it.'

'And Ben shouldn't have grabbed it from you. But that doesn't give you the right to bite him.'

'I was playing with it.'

'If you're playing with something and someone tries to grab it you have to shout and tell Jackie or Bella or Susie.'

'You said it's wrong to shout.'

'It's OK to shout if you're really, really cross. But you're not allowed to bite. Or to hit someone. Because you don't want other people to bite you or hit you, do you?'

'Ben bites people,' said Jacob.

'But you don't want to be like Ben.'

'Can I have my yoghurt now?'

'Not until you understand that biting people is a bad thing to do.'

'I understand,' said Jacob.

'Saying you understand is not the same thing as understanding.'

'But he tried to grab my tractor.'

Ray came in at this point and made the technically correct suggestion that it was unhelpful to hug Jacob while she was telling him off, and she was able to demonstrate immediately a situation where you were allowed to shout at someone if you were really, really cross.

Ray remained infuriatingly calm until Jacob told him not to make Mummy angry because 'You're not my real daddy', at which point he walked into the kitchen and snapped the breadboard into two pieces.

Jacob fixed her with a thirty-five-year-old stare and said, tartly, 'I'm going to eat my yoghurt now,' then went off to consume it in front of *Thomas the Tank Engine*.

The following morning she cancelled her dentist's appointment and spent her day off taking Jacob into the office where he acted like a demented chimp while she and Patsy inserted five thousand erratum slips. By lunchtime he'd taken the chain off Aidan's bike, emptied a card index file and spilled hot chocolate into his shoes.

Come Friday, for the first time in two years she was genuinely relieved when Graham arrived to take him off her hands for forty-eight hours.

Ray headed out to play five-a-side on Saturday morning and she made the mistake of attempting to clean the house. She was manhandling the sofa to get at the fluff and slime and toy-parts underneath when something tore in her lower back. Suddenly she was in a great deal of pain and walking like the butler in a vampire movie.

Ray microwaved some supper and they attempted an orthopaedic, low-impact shag but the ibuprofen seemed to have rendered her numb in all the unhelpful places.

On Sunday she gave in and retired to the sofa, keeping the crap mother guilt at bay with Cary Grant videos.

At six Graham turned up with Jacob.

Ray was in the shower so she let them in herself and tottered back to the chair in the kitchen.

Graham asked what was wrong but Jacob was too busy telling her what a wonderful time they'd had at the Natural History Museum.

'And there were ... there were skellingtons of elephants and rhinoceroses and ... and ... the dinosaurs were ghost dinosaurs.'

'They were repainting one of the rooms,' said Graham. 'Everything was under dust sheets.'

'And Daddy said I could stay up late. And we had ... we had ... we had eggy. And toast. And I helped. And I gotted a chocolate stegosaurus. From the museum. And there was a dead squirrel. In Daddy's ... Daddy's garden. It had worms. In its eyes.'

Katie held her arms out. 'Are you going to give your mummy a big hug?'

But Jacob was in full flow. 'And ... and ... and we went on a double-decker bus and I keeped the tickets.'

Graham crouched down. 'Hang on a tick, little man,

I think your mummy's hurt herself.' He put a finger to Jacob's lips and turned to Katie. 'Are you OK?'

'Wrecked my back. Moving the sofa.'

Graham gave Jacob a serious look. 'You be good to your mummy, all right. Don't go giving her the run-around. Promise?'

Jacob looked at Katie. 'Is your back not comfy?'

'Not very. But a hug from my Monkey Boy would make it feel a lot better.'

Jacob didn't move.

Graham got to his feet. 'Well, it's getting late.'

Jacob began to wail, 'I don't want Daddy to go.'

Graham ruffled his hair, 'Sorry, Buster. Can't be helped, I'm afraid.'

'Come on, Jacob.' Katie held her arms out again. 'Let me give you a cuddle.'

But Jacob was working himself up into a state of truly operatic despair, punching the air and kicking out at the nearest chair. 'Not go. Not go.'

Graham tried to hold him, if only to stop him hurting himself. 'Hey, hey, hey . . .' Normally he would have left. They'd learned the hard way. But normally she could have scooped Jacob into her arms and hung onto him while Graham beat a retreat.

Jacob stamped his feet. 'Nobody . . . Nobody listens . . . I want . . . I hate . . .'

After three or four minutes Ray appeared in the doorway with a towel round his waist. She was past caring what he might say and how Graham might react. He walked over to Jacob, hoisted him over his shoulder and disappeared.

There wasn't time to react. They just stared at the empty door and listened to the screaming getting fainter as Ray and Jacob made their way upstairs.

Graham got to his feet. She thought for a moment that he was going to make some caustic comment and she wasn't sure she could handle that. But he said, 'I'll make some tea,' and it was the kindest thing he'd said to her in a long time.

'Thanks.'

He put the kettle on. 'You're giving me a weird look.'

'The shirt. It's the one I bought you for Christmas.'

'Yeh. Shit. Sorry. I didn't mean to . . .'

'No. I wasn't trying to . . .' She was crying.

'Are you all right?' He reached out to touch her but stopped himself.

'I'm fine. Sorry.'

'Are things going OK?' asked Graham.

'We're getting married.' She was crying properly now. 'Oh crap. I shouldn't be . . .'

He gave her a tissue. 'That's great news.'

'I know.' She blew her nose messily. 'And you? What about you?'

'Oh, nothing much.'

'Tell me,' said Katie.

'I was seeing someone from work.' He took away

her soggy tissue and gave her a fresh one. 'It didn't work out. I mean, she was great, but . . . She wore this swimming cap in the bath to keep her hair dry.'

He took out some fig rolls and they talked about the safe stuff. Ray putting his foot in it with Jamie. Graham's gran modelling for a knitwear catalogue.

After ten minutes he made his excuses. She was sad. It surprised her and he paused just long enough to suggest that he felt the same. There was a brief moment during which one of them might have said something inappropriate. He cut it short.

'You look after yourself, OK?' He kissed her gently on the top of the head and left.

She sat quietly for a few more minutes. Jacob had stopped crying. She realised she hadn't felt the pain while she and Graham had been talking. It was back with a vengeance now. She swigged two more ibuprofen with a glass of water then shuffled upstairs. They were in Jacob's room. She stopped outside and glanced round the door.

Jacob was lying on the bed, face down, looking at the wall. Ray was sitting next to him, patting his bottom and singing 'Ten Green Bottles' very quietly and completely out of tune.

Katie was crying again. And she didn't want Jacob to see. Or Ray for that matter. So she turned and silently walked back down to the kitchen.

9

ON THURSDAY GEORGE announced that he'd booked
the marquee firm and arranged a meeting with two
caterers. This from a man who forgot his children's
birthdays. She was so surprised she didn't even complain about the lack of consultation.

Later that evening a sinister voice in her head
began to ask whether he was making her dispensable.
Ready for when she moved out. Or when he told her
to go.

Yet when the day of the dinner with David rolled
around he was unexpectedly cheerful. He spent the day
shopping and making risotto in the time-honoured
male way, removing all the utensils from the drawers
and laying them out like surgical instruments, then
decanting all the ingredients into small bowls to maxi-
mise the washing-up.

She still couldn't shake the idea that he was planning some kind of showdown, and as the tension rose

during the afternoon she found herself toying with the idea of faking some kind of illness. When the door-bell finally rang just after half seven she ran down the landing, trying to get to the door first and tripped on the loose carpet, twisting her ankle.

By the time she reached the bottom of the stairs, George was standing in the hallway wiping his hands on his stripy apron, and David was handing him a bot-tle of wine and a bunch of flowers.

David noticed her hobbling a little. 'Are you OK?' Instinctively he moved to comfort her, then caught himself and stepped back.

Jean put her hand on George's arm and bent down to rub her ankle. It didn't hurt a great deal, but she wanted to avoid David's eye, and the fear that he might have given something away in that fraction of a second made her feel light-headed.

'Is it bad?' asked George. Thankfully he seemed to have noticed nothing.

'Not too bad,' said Jean.

'You should sit down and put your foot up,' said David. 'To prevent it swelling.' He took the flowers and wine back so that George could help her.

'I'm still in the middle of cooking,' said George. 'Why don't I sit you two down with a glass of wine in the living room?'

'No,' said Jean, a little too firmly. She paused to calm herself. 'We'll come into the kitchen with you.'

George installed them at the table, pulled out a third chair for Jean's ankle, which she didn't really need, filled two wine glasses and returned to grating Parmesan.

It was always going to be a strange occasion, whoever their guest was. George didn't like other people in his kennel. So she assumed the conversation would be stilted. Whenever she dragged him along to parties she would invariably find him standing disconsolately in a circle of men, as they talked about rugby and tax returns, wearing a pained expression on his face, as if he was suffering from a headache. She hoped, at least, that David would be able to fill any silences.

But to her surprise, it was George who did most of the talking. He seemed genuinely excited to have company. The two men congratulated themselves about the decline in Shepherds' fortunes since their departure. They talked about trekking holidays in France. David talked about his gliding. George talked about his fear of flying. David suggested that learning to glide might cure the problem. George said that David clearly underestimated his fear of flying. David confessed to a snake phobia. George asked him to imagine an anaconda in his lap for a couple of hours. David laughed and said George had a point.

Jean's fear ebbed away and was replaced by something odder but equally uncomfortable. It was ridiculous but she didn't want them to be getting on this well. George was warmer and funnier than he was when they were alone together. And David seemed more ordinary.

Was this how they'd been at work? And if so, why had George not mentioned David once since leaving the company? She began to feel rather guilty for having painted David such a bleak picture of her home life.

By the time they decamped to the dining room George and David seemed to have more in common with one another than she had with either of them. It was like being back at school again. Watching your best friend striking up a relationship with another child and being left out in the cold.

She kept muscling into the conversation, trying to claw back some of that attention. But she kept getting it wrong. Sounding far too interested in *Great Expectations* when she'd only seen the TV series. Being too rude about George's previous culinary disasters when the risotto was actually very good. It was tiring. And in the end it seemed easier to take a back seat, leave them to do the talking and give her opinion when asked.

Only at one point did George seem lost for words. David was talking about Martin Donnelly's wife having to go into hospital for tests. She turned round and saw George sitting with his head between his knees. Her first thought was that he'd poisoned everyone with his cooking and was about to vomit. But he sat back, wincing and rubbing his leg, apologised for the interruption, then headed off to do a circuit of the kitchen to ease a muscle spasm.

By the end of the meal he'd drunk an entire bottle of red wine and turned into something of a comic.

'At the risk of boring Jean with an old story, a couple of weeks later we got our photos back. Except they weren't our photos. They were photos of some young man and his girlfriend. In the altogether. Jamie suggested we write *Do you want an enlargement?* on the back before we returned them.'

Over coffee David talked about Mina and the children, and as they stood on the steps watching him drive away on a little cloud of pink smoke, George said, 'You wouldn't ever leave me, would you?'

'Of course not,' said Jean.

She expected him to put an arm round her, at the very least. But he just clapped his hands together, said, 'Right. Washing up,' and headed back inside as if this were simply the next part of the fun.

10

JAMIE PARKED ROUND the corner from Katie's house and composed himself.

You never did escape, of course.

School might have been shit, but at least it was simple. If you could remember your nine-times table, steer clear of Greg Pattershall and draw cartoons of Mrs Cox with fangs and batwings you pretty much had it sorted.

None of which got you very far at thirty-three.

What they failed to teach you at school was that the whole business of being human just got messier and more complicated as you got older.

You could tell the truth, be polite, take everyone's feelings into consideration and still have to deal with other people's shit. At nine or ninety.

He met Daniel at college. And at first it was a relief to find someone who wasn't shagging everything in sight now they were away from home. Then, when the thrill of having a steady boyfriend faded, he realised he was living with a bird-watching Black Sabbath fan and the horrifying thought occurred to him that he might be cut from the same cloth, that even being a sexual pariah in the eyes of the good burghers of Peterborough had failed to make him interesting or cool.

He'd tried celibacy. The only problem was the lack of sex. After a couple of months you'd settle for anything and find yourself being sucked off behind a large shrub at the top of the Heath, which was fine until you came, and the fairy dust evaporated and you realised Prince Charming had a lisp and a weird mole on his ear. And there were Sunday evenings when reading a book was like pulling teeth, so you ate a tin of sweetened condensed milk with a spoon in front of *French and Saunders* and something toxic seeped under the sash windows and you began to wonder what in God's name the point of it all was.

He didn't want much. Companionship. Shared interests. A bit of space.

The problem was that no one else knew what they wanted.

He'd managed three half-decent relationships since Daniel. But something always changed after six months, after a year. They wanted more. Or less. Nicholas thought they should spice up their love life by sleeping with other people. Steven thought he should move in. With his cats. And Olly slid into a deep depression after his father died so that Jamie turned from a partner into some kind of social worker.

Fast-forward six years and he and Shona were in the pub after work when she said that she was going to try and fix him up with a cute builder who was decorating the Princes Avenue flats. But she was drunk and Jamie couldn't imagine how Shona, of all people, had correctly ascertained the sexual orientation of a working-class person. So he forgot about the conversation completely until they were over in Muswell Hill, and Jamie was doing a walk-through, zapping the interior measurements and having a vague sexual fantasy about the guy painting the kitchen when Shona came in and said, 'Tony, this is Jamie. Jamie, this is Tony,' and Tony turned round and smiled and Jamie realised that Shona was, in truth, a wiser old bird than he'd given her credit for.

She slipped away and he and Tony talked about property development and cycling and Tunisia, with a glancing reference to the ponds on the Heath to make absolutely sure they were singing from the same hymn sheet, and Tony pulled a printed business card from his back pocket and said, 'If you ever need anything . . .', which Jamie did, very much.

He waited a couple of nights so as not to seem desperate, then met him for a drink in Highgate. Tony told a story about bathing naked with friends off Studland and how they had to empty wastebins and turn the black bags into rudimentary kilts to hitch back to Poole after their clothes were nicked. And Jamie explained how he reread *The Lord of the Rings* every year. But it felt right. The difference. Like two interlocking pieces of jigsaw.

After an Indian meal they went back to Jamie's flat and Tony did at least two things to him on the sofa that no one had ever done to him before, then came back and did them again the following evening, and suddenly life became very good indeed.

It made him uncomfortable, being dragged along to Chelsea matches. It made him uncomfortable, ringing in sick so they could fly to Edinburgh for a long weekend. But Jamie needed someone who made him uncomfortable. Because getting too comfortable was the thin end of a wedge whose thick end involved him turning into his father.

And, of course, if a sash window broke or the kitchen needed a new coat of paint, well, that made up for the Clash at high volume and work boots in the sink.

They had arguments. You couldn't spend a day in Tony's company without an argument. But Tony thought they were all part of the fun of human relationships. Tony also liked sex as a way of making up afterwards. In fact, Jamie sometimes wondered whether Tony only started arguments so they could make up afterwards. But the sex was too good to complain.

And now they were at one another's throats over a wedding. A wedding that had bugger all to do with Tony and, to be honest, not a lot to do with Jamie.

There was a crick in his neck.

He lifted his head and realised that he'd been leaning his forehead on the steering wheel for the last five minutes.

He got out of the car. Tony was right. He couldn't make Katie change her mind. It was guilt, really. Not having been there to listen.

There was no use worrying about that now. He had to make amends. Then he could stop feeling guilty.

Fuck. He should have bought cake.

It didn't matter. Cake wasn't really the point.

Half past two. They'd have the rest of the afternoon before Ray got home. Tea. Chat. Piggybacks and aeroplanes for Jacob. If they were lucky he'd take a nap and they could have a decent talk.

He walked up the path and rang the bell.

The door opened and he found the hallway blocked by Ray wearing paint-spattered overalls and holding some kind of electric drill.

'So, that's two of us taking the day off,' said Ray. 'Gas leak at the office.' He held up the drill and pressed the button so that it whizzed a bit. 'You heard the news, then.'

'I did.' Jamie nodded. 'Congratulations.'

Congratulations?

Ray extended a beefy paw and Jamie found his own hand sucked into its gravitational field.

'That's a relief,' said Ray. 'Thought you might've come to punch my lights out.'

Jamie managed a laugh. 'It wouldn't be much of a fight, would it.'

'No.' Ray's laughter was louder and more relaxed. 'You coming in?'

'Sure. Is Katie around?'

'Sainsbury's. With Jacob. I'm fixing stuff. Should be back in half an hour.'

Before Jamie could think of an appointment he might have been *en route* to Ray closed the door behind him. 'Have a cup of coffee while I stick the door back on this cupboard.'

'I'd prefer tea, if that's OK,' said Jamie. The word *tea* did not sound manly.

'I reckon we can do tea.'

Jamie sat himself down at the kitchen table feeling not unlike he had felt in the back of that Cessna before the ill-fated parachute jump.

'Glad you came.' Ray put the drill down and washed his hands. 'Something I wanted to ask you.'

A horrifying image came to mind of Ray patiently soaking up the hate-waves over the past eight months, waiting for the moment when he and Jamie were finally alone together.

He put the kettle on, leaned against the sink, pushed

his hands deep into his trouser pockets and stared at the floor. 'Do you reckon I should marry Katie?'

Jamie wasn't sure he'd heard this correctly. And there were certain questions you just didn't answer in case you'd got the wrong end of a very big stick (Neil Turley in the showers after football that summer, for example).

'You know her better than me.' Ray had the look on his face that Katie had at eight when she was trying to bend spoons with mind power. 'Do you . . . ? I mean, this is going to sound bloody stupid, but do you think she actually loves me?'

This question Jamie heard with horrible clarity. He was now sitting at the door of the Cessna with four thousand feet of nothing between his feet and Hertfordshire. In five seconds he'd be dropping like a stone, passing out and filling his helmet with sick.

Ray looked up. There was a silence in the kitchen like the silence in an isolated barn in a horror film.

Deep breath. Tell the truth. Be polite. Take Ray's feelings into consideration. Deal with the shit. 'I don't know. I really don't. Katie and I haven't talked that much over the last year. I've been busy, she's been spending time with you . . .' He trailed off.

Ray seemed to have shrunk to the size of an entirely normal human being. 'She gets so bloody angry.'

Jamie badly wanted the tea, if only for something to hold.

'I mean, I get angry,' said Ray. He put teabags into two mugs and poured the water. 'Tell me about it. But Katie . . .'

'I know,' said Jamie.

Was Ray listening? It was hard to tell. Perhaps he just needed someone to aim the words at.

'It's like this black cloud,' said Ray.

How did Ray do it? One moment he was dominating a room the way a lorry would. Next minute he was down a hole and asking you for help. Why couldn't he suffer in a way they could all enjoy from a safe distance?

'It's not you,' said Jamie.

Ray looked up. 'Really?'

'Well, maybe it is you.' Jamie paused. 'But she gets angry with us, too.'

'Right.' Ray bent down and slid rawlplugs into four holes he'd drilled inside the cupboard. 'Right.' He stood and removed the teabags. The atmosphere slackened a little and Jamie began looking forward to a conversation about football or loft insulation. But when Ray placed the tea in front of Jamie he said, 'So, what about you and Tony?'

'What do you mean?'

'I mean, what about you and Tony?'

'I'm not sure I understand,' said Jamie.

'You love him, right?'

Jesus H. Christ. If Ray made a habit of asking questions like this, no wonder Katie got angry.

Ray slid some more rawlplugs into the door of the cupboard. 'I mean, Katie said you were lonely. Then you met this chap and . . . you know . . . Bingo.'

Was it humanly possible to feel more ill at ease than he did at this moment? His hands were shaking and there were ripples in the tea like in *Jurassic Park* when the T-rex was approaching.

'Katie says he's a decent bloke.'

'Why are we talking about me and Tony?'

'You have arguments, right?' said Ray.

'Ray, it's none of your business whether we have arguments or not.'

Dear God. He was telling Ray to back off. Jamie never told people to back off. He felt like he did when Robbie North threw that can of petrol onto the bonfire, knowing that a bad thing was about to happen very soon.

'Sorry.' Ray held up his hands. 'This gay stuff's all a bit foreign to me.'

'It's got absolutely nothing to do with . . . Jeez.' Jamie put his tea down in case he spilled it. He felt a little dizzy. He took a deep breath and spoke slowly. 'Yes. Tony and I have arguments. Yes, I love Tony. And . . .'

I love Tony.

He'd said he loved Tony. He'd said it to Ray. He hadn't even said it to himself.

Did he love Tony?

Christ alive.

Ray said, 'Look . . .'

'No. Wait.' Jamie put his head in his hands.

It was the life/school/other people thing all over again. You turned up at your sister's house with the best of intentions, you found yourself talking to someone who had failed to grasp the most basic rules of human conversation and suddenly there was a motorway pile-up in your head.

He steeled himself. 'Perhaps we should just talk about football.'

'Football?' asked Ray.

'Man stuff.' The bizarre idea came to him that they could be friends. Maybe not friends. But people who could rub along together. Christmas in the trenches and all that.

'Are you taking the piss?' asked Ray.

Jamie breathed deeply. 'Katie's lovely. But she's hard work. You couldn't give her a biscuit against her will. If she's marrying you it's because she wants to marry you.'

The drill slid off the counter and hit the stone floor tiles and it sounded like a mortar shell going off.

11

RAY TURNED TO Katie in bed and said, 'Are you sure you want to marry me?'

'Of course I want to marry you.'

'You'd tell me if you changed your mind, yeh?'

'Jeez, Ray,' said Katie. 'What's all this about?'

'You wouldn't go through with it just because we'd told everyone?'

'Ray . . .'

'Do you love me?' he asked.

'Why are you talking like this all of a sudden?'

'Do you love me like you loved Graham?'

'No, actually, I don't,' said Katie.

For a second she could see real pain on his face. 'I was infatuated with Graham. I thought he was God's gift. I couldn't see straight. And when I found out what he was really like . . .' She put her hand on the side of Ray's face. 'I know you. I know all the things that are wonderful about you. I know all your faults. And I still want to marry you.'

'So, what are my faults?'

This wasn't her job. He was the one who was meant to do the consoling. 'Come here.' She pulled his head onto her chest.

'I love you so much.' He sounded tiny.

'Don't worry. I'm not going to ditch you at the altar.'

'I'm sorry. I'm being stupid.'

'It's wedding nerves.' She ran her hand over the little hairs on his upper arm. 'You remember Emily?'

'Yeh?'

'Threw up in the vestry.'

'Shit.'

'They had to send her up the aisle with this massive bouquet to hide the stain. Barry's dad assumed the smell was Roddy. You know, after their stag night.'

They fell asleep and were woken at four by Jacob crying, 'Mummy, Mummy, Mummy . . .'

Ray started to get out of bed but she insisted on going.

When she got to his room Jacob was still half asleep, trying to curl away from a big orange diarrhoea-stain in the centre of the bed.

'Come here, little squirrel.' She lifted him to his feet and his sleepy head flopped against her shoulder.

'It's all . . . all sort of . . . It's wet.'

'I know. I know.' She carefully peeled off his pyjama trousers, rolling them up so that the mess was on the inside then throwing them into the hallway. 'Let's clean you up, Baby Biscuits.' She grabbed a nappy bag and a fresh nappy and pack of wet-wipes from the drawer and gently cleaned his bottom.

She put the fresh nappy on, extracted a fresh pair of pyjama trousers from the basket and guided his clumsy feet into the legs. 'There. That feels better, doesn't it.'

She flicked the Winnie the Pooh duvet over to check that it was clean, then bundled it onto the carpet. 'You lie down for a second while I sort the bed out.'

Jacob cried as she lowered him to the floor. 'Don't want to . . . Let me . . .' But when she laid his head on the duvet, his thumb slipped into his mouth and his eyes closed again.

She tied the nappy bag and threw it into the bin. She stripped the bed, threw the dirty sheets into the hallway and turned the mattress over. She grabbed a new set of sheets from the cupboard and pressed them to her face. God, it was lovely, the furriness of thick, worn cotton and the scent of washing powder. She made the bed, tucking the edges in tight so that it was smooth and flat.

She plumped the pillow, bent over and hoisted Jacob up.

'My tummy hurts.'

She held him on her lap. 'We'll get you some Calpol in a minute.'

'Pink medicine,' said Jacob.

She wrapped her arms around him. She didn't get enough of this. Not when he was conscious. Thirty seconds at most. Then it was helicopters and bouncy-bouncy on the sofa. True, it made her proud, seeing him in a circle listening to Bella read a book at nursery, or watching him talk to other children in the playground. But she missed the way he was once a part of her body, the way she could make everything better just by folding herself around him. Even now she could picture him leaving home, the distance opening up already, her baby becoming his own little person.

'I miss my daddy.'

'He's asleep upstairs.'

'My real daddy,' said Jacob.

She put her hand around his head and kissed his hair. 'I miss him too, sometimes.'

'But he's not coming back.'

'No. He's not coming back.'

Jacob was crying quietly.

'But I'll never leave you. You know that, don't you.' She wiped the snot from his nose with the arm of her T-shirt and rocked him.

She looked up at the Bob the Builder height chart

and the sailing boat mobile turning silently in the half-dark. Somewhere under the floor a water pipe clanked.

Jacob stopped crying. 'Can I have a polar bear drink tomorrow?'

She pushed the hair out of his eyes. 'I'm not sure whether you'll be fit for nursery tomorrow.' His eyes moistened. 'But if you are, we'll get a polar bear drink on the way home, OK?'

'All right.'

'But if you have a polar bear drink, you won't be able to have any pudding for supper. Is that a deal?'

'That's a deal.'

'Now, let's get you some Calpol.'

She laid him down on the clean sheets and got the bottle and the syringe from the bathroom.

'Open wide.'

He was almost asleep now. She squirted the medicine into his mouth, wiped a dribble from his chin with the tip of her finger and licked it clean.

She kissed his cheek. 'I have to go back to bed now, little boy.'

But he didn't want to let go of her hand. And she didn't want him to let go. She sat watching him sleep for a few minutes, then lay down beside him.

This made up for everything, the tiredness, the tantrums, the fact that she hadn't read a novel in six months. This was how Ray made her feel.

This was how Ray was meant to make her feel.

She stroked Jacob's head. He was a million miles away, dreaming of raspberry ice cream and earth-moving machinery and the Cretaceous period.

The next thing she knew it was morning and Jacob was running in and out of the room in his Spiderman outfit.

'Come on, love.' Ray pushed the hair away from her face. 'There's a fry-up waiting for you downstairs.'

After nursery she and Jacob got home late on account of having stopped to get the polar bear drink, and Ray was already back from the office.

'Graham rang,' he said.

'What about?'

'Didn't tell me.'

'Anything important?' asked Katie.

'Didn't ask. Said he'd try again later.'

One mysterious call from Graham a day was pretty much Ray's limit. So, after putting Jacob to bed, she used the phone in the bedroom.

'It's Katie.'

'Hey, you rang back.'

'So, what's the big secret?'

'No big secret, I'm just worried about you. Which didn't seem the kind of message to leave with Ray.'

'I'm sorry. I wasn't in terribly good shape when you turned up the other evening, what with my back and everything.'

'Are you talking to anyone?' asked Graham.

'You mean, like, professionally?'

'No, I mean just talking.'

'Of course I'm talking,' said Katie.

'You know what I mean.'

'Graham. Look . . .'

'If you want me to butt out,' said Graham, 'I'll butt out. And I don't want to cast any aspersions on Ray. I really don't. I just wondered whether you wanted to meet up for a coffee and a chat. We're still friends, right? OK, maybe we're not friends. But you seemed like you might need to get stuff off your chest. And I don't necessarily mean bad stuff.' He paused. 'Also, I really enjoyed talking to you the other night.'

God knows what had happened to him. She hadn't heard him sounding this solicitous in years. If it was jealousy it didn't sound like jealousy. Perhaps the woman with the swimming cap had broken his heart.

She stopped herself. It was an unkind thought. People changed. He was being kind. And he was right. She wasn't talking enough.

'I'm finishing early on Wednesday. I could see you for an hour before I pick Jacob up.'

'Brilliant.'

12

THE CAR WAS parked outside. Consequently he was surprised and a little disappointed to find the house empty. On the other hand, being in his own hallway was a comfort. The pig-shaped notepad on the phone table. The faint scent of toast. That piny stuff Jean used to clean the carpets. He put his rucksack down and walked into the kitchen.

He was putting the kettle on when he noticed that one of the chairs was lying on the floor. He bent down and set it back on its feet.

He found himself thinking briefly of ghost ships, everything precisely as it was when disaster struck, half-eaten meals, unfinished diary entries.

Then he stopped himself. It was just a chair. He filled the kettle, plugged it in, placed his hands flat on the Formica work surface, exhaled slowly and let the crazy thoughts slip away.

And this was when he heard the noise, from

somewhere above his head, like someone moving heavy furniture. He assumed it was Jean at first. But it was a sound he had never heard in the house before, a rhythmic bumping, almost mechanical.

He very nearly called out. Then he decided not to. He wanted to know what was happening before he announced his presence. He might need the element of surprise.

He walked into the hallway and began climbing the stairs. When he reached the top he realised that the noise was coming from one of the bedrooms.

He walked down the landing. The door of Katie's old room was closed, but his and Jean's door was standing slightly ajar. This was where the noise was coming from.

Glancing down he saw the four large marble eggs in the fruit bowl on the chest. He took the black one and cradled it in his hand. It wasn't much of a weapon but it was extremely dense and he felt safer holding it. He tossed it a couple of times, letting it fall heavily back into the palm of his hand.

It was highly possible that he was about to confront a drug-addict rifling through their drawers. He should have been scared, but the morning's activities seemed to have emptied that particular tank.

He stepped up to the door and pushed it gently open.

Two people were having sexual intercourse on the bed.

He had never seen two people having sexual intercourse before, not in real life. It did not look attractive. His first impulse was to step swiftly away to save embarrassment. Then he remembered that it was his room. And his bed.

He was about to ask the two of them loudly what in God's name they thought they were playing at when he noticed that they were old people. Then the woman made the noise he had heard from downstairs. And it wasn't just a woman. It was Jean.

The man was raping her.

He raised the fist containing the marble egg and stepped forward again, but she said, 'Yes, yes, yes, yes,' and he could see now that the naked man between her legs was David Symmonds.

Without warning the house tilted to one side. He stepped backwards and put his hand on the doorframe to prevent himself falling over.

Time passed. Precisely how much time passed it was difficult to say. Something between five seconds and two minutes.

He did not feel very well.

He pulled the door back to its original position and steadied himself on the banisters. He silently repositioned the marble egg in the bowl and waited for the house to return to its normal angle, like a big ship in a long swell.

When it had done so he made his way down the

stairs, picked up his rucksack, stepped through the front door and pulled it shut behind him.

There was a sound in his head like the sound he might have heard if he were lying on a railway line and an express train were passing over him.

He began walking. Walking was good. Walking cleared the head.

A blue estate car drove past.

This time it was the pavement which was tilting to one side. He came to a halt, bent over and was sick at the foot of a lamp post.

Maintaining his position to avoid messing his trousers, he fished an elderly tissue from his pocket and wiped his mouth. It seemed wrong, somehow, to dump the tissue in the street and he was about to put it back in his pocket when the weight of his rucksack shifted unexpectedly, he put his hand out to grab the lamp post, missed and rolled into a hedge.

He was buying a cottage pie and a fruit salad in Knutsford South Services on the M6 when he was woken by the sound of a dog barking and opened his eyes to find himself staring at a large area of overcast sky fringed by leaves and twigs.

He gazed at the overcast sky for a while.

There was a strong smell of vomit.

It became slowly clear that he was lying in a hedge. There was a rucksack on his back. He remembered now. He had been sick in the street and his wife was having sexual intercourse with another man a couple of hundred yards away.

He did not want to be seen lying in a hedge.

It took him several seconds to remember precisely how one commanded one's limbs. When he did, he removed a branch from his hair, slipped his arms free of the rucksack and got gingerly to his feet.

A woman was standing on the far side of the street watching him with mild interest, as if he were an animal in a safari park. He counted to five, took a deep breath and hoisted the rucksack onto his shoulders.

He took a tentative step.

He took another, slightly less tentative step.

He could do it.

He began walking towards the main road.

13

JAMIE HOOVERED THE carpets and cleaned the bathroom. He thought briefly about washing the cushion
covers but, frankly, Tony wouldn't notice if they were
covered in mud.

The following afternoon he cut short the visit to
the Creighton Avenue flats, rang the office to say he
could be contacted on his mobile, then went home
via Tesco's.

Salmon, then strawberries. Enough to show he'd
made an effort but not enough to make him feel too
fat for sex. He put a bottle of Pouilly Fumé in the
fridge and a vase of tulips on the dining table.

He felt stupid. He was getting worked up about los-
ing Katie, and doing nothing to hang onto the most
important person in his life.

He and Tony should be living together. He should
be coming home to lit windows and the sound of
unfamiliar music. He should be lying in bed on

Saturday mornings, smelling bacon and hearing the clink of crockery through the wall.

He was going to take Tony to the wedding. All that bollocks about provincial bigotry. It was himself he was scared of. Getting old. Making choices. Being committed.

It would be ghastly. Of course it would be ghastly. But it didn't matter what the neighbours thought. It didn't matter if his mother fussed over Tony like a lost son. It didn't matter if his father tied himself in knots over bedroom arrangements. It didn't matter if Tony insisted on a slow snog to Lionel Richie's 'Three Times a Lady'.

He wanted to share his life with Tony. The good stuff and the crap stuff.

He took a deep breath and felt, for several seconds, as if he was standing not on the pine floor of his kitchen but on some deserted Scottish headland, the surf thundering and the wind in his hair. Noble. Taller.

He went to the bathroom and showered and felt the remains of something dirty being rinsed away and sent spinning down the plughole.

He was having a shirt selection crisis when the doorbell rang. He plumped for the faded orange denim and went down the hall.

When he opened the door his first thought was that Tony had received some bad news. About his father, perhaps.

'What's the matter?'

Tony took a deep breath.

'Hey. Come inside,' said Jamie.

Tony didn't move. 'We need to talk.'

'Come inside and talk.'

Tony didn't want to come inside. He suggested they walk to the park at the end of the road. Jamie grabbed his keys.

It happened next to the little red bin for dog shit.

Tony said, 'It's over.'

'What?'

'Us. It's over.'

'But . . .'

'You don't really want to be with me,' said Tony.

'I do,' said Jamie.

'OK. Maybe you want to be with me. But you don't want to be with me enough. This stupid wedding. It's made me realise . . . Jesus, Jamie. Am I just not good enough for your parents? Or am I not good enough for you?'

'I love you.' Why was this happening now? It was so unfair, so idiotic.

Tony looked at him. 'You don't know what love is.'

'I do.' He sounded like Jacob.

Tony's expression didn't change. 'Loving someone means taking the risk that they might fuck up your nicely ordered little life. And you don't want to fuck up your nicely ordered little life, do you?'

'Have you met someone else?'

'You're not listening to a word I'm saying.'

He should have explained. The salmon. The hoovering. The words were there in his head. He just couldn't get them out. He hurt too much. And there was something sickly and comforting about the thought of going back to the house alone, smashing the tulips from the table, then retiring to the sofa to drink the bottle of wine on his own.

'I'm sorry, Jamie. I really am. You're a nice guy.' Tony put his hands into his pockets to show that there would be no final embrace. 'I hope you find someone who makes you feel that way.'

He turned and walked off.

Jamie stood in the park for several minutes, then went back to the flat, smashed the tulips from the table, uncorked the wine, took it to the sofa and wept.

14

WHEN DAVID HAD gone Jean wandered down to the kitchen in her dressing gown.

Everything glowed a little. The flowers in the wallpaper. The clouds piled in the sky at the end of the garden like snowdrifts.

She made a coffee and a ham sandwich and took a couple of paracetamol for her knee.

And the glow began to fade a little.

Upstairs, when David was holding her, it seemed possible. Putting all of this behind her. Starting a new life. But now that he was gone it seemed preposterous. A wicked idea. Something people did on television.

She looked at the wall clock. She looked at the bills in the toast rack and the cheese plate with the ivy pattern.

She suddenly saw her whole life laid out, like pictures in a photo album. Her and George standing outside the church in Daventry, the wind blowing the

leaves off the trees like orange confetti, the real celebration only starting when they left their families
behind the following morning and drove to Devon in
George's bottle-green Austin.

Stuck in hospital for a month after Katie was born.
George coming in every day with fish and chips. Jamie
on his red tricycle. The house in Clarendon Lane. Ice on
the windows that first winter and frozen flannels you
had to crack. It all seemed so solid, so normal, so good.

You looked at someone's life like that and you never
saw what was missing.

She washed up her sandwich plate and stacked it
in the rack. The house seemed suddenly rather drab.
The scale round the base of the taps. The cracks in
the soap. The sad cactus.

Perhaps she wanted too much. Perhaps everyone
wanted too much these days. The washer-dryer. The
bikini figure. The feelings you had when you were
twenty-one.

She headed upstairs and, as she changed into her
clothes, she could feel herself slipping back into her
old self.

*I want to go to bed with you at night and I want to
wake up with you in the morning.*

David didn't understand. You could say no. But you
couldn't have that kind of conversation and pretend
it never happened.

She missed George.

15

KATIE AND GRAHAM didn't talk about Ray. They didn't even talk about the wedding. They talked about *Bridget Jones* and the petrol tanker hanging off the Westway on the TV news that morning and the truly bizarre hair of the woman in the far corner of the café.

It was exactly what Katie needed. Like putting on an old jumper. The good fit. The comforting smell.

She'd just asked the waitress for the bill, however, when she looked up and saw Ray coming into the café and walking towards them. For half a second she wondered whether there had been some kind of emergency. Then she saw the look on his face and she was livid.

Ray stopped beside the table and looked down at Graham.

'What's this about?' Katie asked.

Ray said nothing.

Graham calmly put seven pound coins on the little stainless steel dish and slid his arms into his jacket. 'I'd better be going.' He stood up. 'Thanks for the chat.'

'I'm really sorry about this.' She turned to Ray. 'For God's sake, Ray. Grow up.'

For one horrible moment she thought Ray was going to hit Graham. But he didn't. He just watched as Graham walked slowly to the door.

'Well, that was charming, Ray. Just charming. How old are you?'

Ray stared at her.

'Are you going to say anything, or are you just going to stand there with that moronic look on your face?'

Ray turned and walked out of the café.

The waitress returned to pick up the little stainless steel dish and Ray appeared on the pavement outside the window. He lifted a wastebin over his head, roared like a deranged vagrant then hurled it down the pavement.

The Red House

COOLING TOWERS AND sewage farms. Finstock, Charlbury, Ascott-under-Wychwood. Seventy miles per hour, the train unzips the fields. Two gun-grey lines beside the river's meander. Flashes of sun on the hammered metal. Something of steam about it, even now. Hogwarts and Adlestrop. The night mail crossing the border. Cheyenne sweeping down from the ridge. Delta blues from the boxcar. Somewhere, those secret points that might just switch and send you curving into a world of uniformed porters and great-aunts and summers at the lake.

Angela leant against the cold window, hypnotised by the power lines as they sagged and were scooped up by the next gantry, over and over and over. Polytunnels like silver mattresses, indecipherable swirls of graffiti on a brick siding. She'd buried her mother six weeks ago. A bearded man in a suit with shiny elbows playing 'Danny Boy' on Northumbrian pipes.

Everything out of kilter, the bandage on the vicar's hand, that woman chasing her windblown hat between the headstones, the dog that belonged to no one. She thought her mother had left the world a long way back, the weekly visits mostly for Angela's own benefit. Boiled mutton, Classic FM and a commode in flesh-coloured plastic. Her death should have been a relief. Then the first spade of earth hit the coffin, a bubble rose in her chest and she realised her mother had been . . . what? a cornerstone? a breakwater?

THE WEEK AFTER the funeral Dominic had been standing at the sink bottle-brushing the green vase. The last of the freak snow was still packed down the side of the shed and the rotary washing line was turning in the wind. Angela came in holding the phone as if it was a mystery object she'd found on the hall table. *That was Richard.*

Dominic upended the vase on the wire rack. *And what did he want?*

He's offered to take us on holiday.

He dried his hands on the tea towel. *Are we talking about your brother, or some entirely different Richard?*

We are indeed talking about my brother.

He really had no idea what to say. Angela and Richard had spent no more than an afternoon in each other's company over the last fifteen years and their meeting at the funeral had seemed perfunctory at best. *Where's the exotic location?*

He's rented a house on the Welsh border. Near Hay-on-Wye.

The fine sandy beaches of Herefordshire. He halved the tea towel and hung it over the radiator.

I said yes.

Well, thanks for the consultation.

Angela paused and held his eye. *Richard knows we can't afford a holiday of our own. I'm not looking forward to it any more than you, but I didn't have a great deal of choice.*

He held up his hands. *Point taken.* They'd had this argument way too many times. *Herefordshire it is, then.*

ORDNANCE SURVEY 161. *The Black Mountains/Y Myn-yddoedd Duon.* Dominic flipped up the pink cover and unfolded the big paper concertina. He had loved maps since he was a boy. Here be monsters. X marks the spot. The edges of the paper browned and scalloped with a burning match, messages flashed from peak to peak using triangles of broken mirror.

He looked sideways at Angela. So hard to remember that girl on the far side of the union bar, her shoulders in that blue summer dress. She disgusted him now, the size and sag of her, the veins on her calves, almost a grandmother. He dreamt of her dying unexpectedly, rediscovering all those freedoms he'd lost twenty years ago. Then he had the same dream five minutes later and he remembered what poor use he'd made of those freedoms first time round and he heard the squeak of trolley wheels and saw the bags of fluid. All those other lives. You never did get to lead them.

He gazed out of the window and saw a narrowboat on the adjacent canal, some bearded pillock at the tiller, pipe, mug of tea. *Ahoy there, matey.* Stupid way to spend a holiday, banging your head every time you stood up. A week in a boat with Richard. Think of that. They were in the middle of nowhere, thank goodness. If it all got too much he could walk up into the hills and yell at the sky. To be honest, it was Angela he was worried about. All that hard-wired sibling friction. Do not return once lit and so forth.

Richard's hair, yes. Now that he thought about it that was where the evil was located, this luxuriant black crest, like the tusks of a bull walrus, a warning to beta males. Or like a separate creature entirely, some alien life form that had pushed suckers into his skull and was using him as a vehicle.

THE CHILDREN SAT opposite. Alex, seventeen, was reading *Main Force* by Andy McNab. Daisy, sixteen, was reading a book called *The Art of Daily Prayer*. Benjy, eight, had swivelled so that his feet were on the headrest and his head was hanging over the edge of the seat, eyes closed. Angela poked his shoulder with the toe of her shoe. *What on earth are you doing?*

I'm on horseback beheading Nazi zombies.

They looked like children from three separate families, Alex the athlete, all shoulders and biceps, off into the wide blue yonder every other weekend, canoeing, mountain-biking, Benjy a kind of boy-liquid which had been poured into whatever space he happened to be occupying, and Daisy . . . Angela wondered if something dreadful had happened to her daughter over the past year, something that might explain the arrogant humility, the way she'd made herself so ostentatiously plain.

They plunged into a tunnel and the windows thumped and clattered. She saw an overweight, middle-aged woman floating out there in the dark for several seconds before she vanished in a blast of sunlight and poplars, and she was back in her body again, dress pinching at the waist, beads of sweat in the small of her back, that train smell, burning dust, hot brakes, the dull reek of the toilets.

CARTER PLACED HIS *boot on the man's shoulder and rolled him over. This couldn't be happening. He'd killed Bunny O'Neil. They'd trained together in the Cairngorms ten years ago. What was an ex-SAS captain doing in the middle of Afghanistan, armed with a black-market Soviet rifle, trying to assassinate a billionaire head of an international construction company?*

*

FURTHER DOWN THE carriage the ticket collector was squatting beside a bird-frail woman with long grey hair and spectacles on a red string. *So you've come on the train with no ticket and no means of payment?* Shaved head, cloudy blue tattoo on his meaty forearm.

Angela wanted to pay for her ticket and save her from this bullying man.

She was trying to pick something invisible from the air with her tiny liver-spotted hands. *I can't . . .*

Is someone meeting you at Hereford? A tenderness in his voice which she hadn't heard the first time. He touched the woman's arm gently to get her attention. *A son, maybe, or a daughter?*

The woman clawed at the air. *I can't quite . . .*

Angela felt a prickle at the corner of her eye and turned away.

RICHARD HAD REMARRIED six months ago, acquiring a step-daughter into the bargain. Angela hadn't gone to the wedding. Edinburgh was a long way, it was term time and they'd never felt like brother and sister, just two people who spoke briefly on the phone every few weeks or so to manage the stages of their mother's decline. She'd met Louisa and Melissa for the first time at the funeral. They looked as if they had been purchased from an exclusive catalogue at some exorbitant price, flawless skin and matching black leather boots. The girl stared at her and didn't look away when Angela caught her eye. Bobbed chestnut hair, black denim skirt almost but not quite too short for a funeral. So much sheen and sneer at sixteen. *Melissa's directing a play at school.* A Midsummer Night's Dream.

Something slightly footballer's wife about Louisa. Angela couldn't picture her going to the theatre or reading a serious book, couldn't imagine the conversations she and Richard might have when they were alone. But his judgement of other people had always been a little wobbly. Ten years married to the Ginger Witch. The presents he bought for the kids when he last visited, so much effort aimed in the wrong direction. Benjy's football annual, Daisy's bracelet. She wondered if he was making a new version of the same mistake, whether she was simply not-Jennifer, and he was another rung on the social ladder.

I'm going to the loo. Benjy stood up. *My bladder is so awesomely full.*

Don't get lost. She touched his sleeve.

You can't get lost on a train.

A sick pervert could strangle you, said Alex, *and throw your body out of a window.*

I'll punch him in the crutch.

Crotch, said Alex.

Critch, crotch, cratch . . . sang Benjy as he made his way up the carriage.

*

Eventually we find that we no longer need silence. We no longer need solitude. We no longer even need words. We can make all our actions holy. We can cook a meal for our family and it becomes prayer. We can go for a walk in the park and it becomes prayer.

Alex photographed a herd of cows. What was the point of being black and white, evolutionarily? He hated real violence. He could still hear the snap of Callum's leg that night in Crouch End. He felt sick when he saw footage from Iraq or Afghanistan. He didn't tell anyone about this. But Andy McNab tamed it by turning it into a cartoon. And now he was thinking about Melissa unzipping that black denim skirt. The word *unzipping* gave him an erection which he covered with the novel. But was it OK fancying your uncle's step-daughter? Some people married their cousins and that was acceptable, unless you both had recessive genes for something bad and your babies came out really fucked up. But girls who went to private school were secretly gagging for it, with their tans and their white knickers that smelt of fabric conditioner. Except she probably wouldn't speak to him, would she, because girls only spoke to twats with floppy hair and skinny jeans. On the other hand, normal service was kind of suspended on holiday and maybe they'd be sharing a bathroom and he'd go in and open the shower cubicle door and squeeze her soapy tits so she moaned.

A MAN IS trapped in a hot flat above the shipyard, caring for a wife who will live out her days in this bed, watching this television. Twin sisters are separated at seven weeks and know nothing of one another, only an absence that walks beside them always on the road. A girl is raped by her mother's boyfriend. A child dies and doesn't die. *Family*, that slippery word, a star to every wandering bark, and everyone sailing under a different sky.

AND THEN THERE was her fourth child, the child no one else could see. Karen, her loved and secret ghost, stillborn all those years ago. Holoprosencephaly. Hox genes failing along the midline of the head. Her little monster, features melted into the centre of her face. They'd told her not to look but she'd looked and screamed at them to take the thing away. Then in the small hours, while Dominic slept and the ward was still, she wanted that tiny damaged body in her arms again, because she could learn to love her, she really could, but the points had switched and Karen had swerved away into the parallel world she glimpsed sometimes from cars and trains, the spiderweb sheds and the gypsy camps, the sidings and the breakers' yards, the world she visited in dreams, stumbling through dogshit and nettles, the air treacly with heat, lured by a girl's voice and the flash of a summer dress. And this coming Thursday would be Karen's eighteenth birthday. Which was what she hated about the countryside, no distraction from the dirty messed-up workings of the heart. *You'll love it*, Dominic had said. *Inbred locals surrounding the house at night with pitchforks and flaming brands*. Not understanding, in the way that he failed to understand so many things these days.

DOMINIC WIPED THE sandwich crumbs from his lip and looked over at Daisy who smiled briefly before returning to her book. She was so much calmer these days, none of the unpredictable tears which spilt out of her last year, making him feel clumsy and useless. It was bollocks, of course, the Jesus stuff, and some of the church people made his flesh crawl. Bad clothes and false cheer. But he was oddly proud, the strength of her conviction, the way she swam so doggedly against the current. If only her real friends hadn't drifted away. But Alex wouldn't look up however long you stared. If he was reading he was reading, if he was running he was running. He'd expected more from having a son. That Oedipal rage between two and four. *Stop hugging Mummy*. Then, from seven to ten, a golden time, filling a buried cashbox with baby teeth and Pokémon cards, camping in the New

Forest, that night the pony opened the zip of their tent and stole their biscuits. He taught Alex how to play the piano, theme tunes arranged in C Major with a single finger in the left hand. *Star Wars*, *Raiders of the Lost Ark*. But he grew bored of the piano and gave Benjy the key to the cashbox and went camping with his friends. Devon, the Peak District.

He wondered sometimes if he loved Daisy not because of the strength of her belief but because of her loneliness, the mess she was making of her life, the way it rhymed with his own.

BEHIND EVERYTHING THERE is a house. Behind everything there is always a house, compared to which every other house is larger or colder or more luxurious. Cladding over thirties brick, a broken greenhouse, rhubarb and rusted cans of Castrol for the mower. At the far end you can peel back the corner of the chicken-wire fence and slip down into the cutting where the trains run to Sheffield every half-hour. The tarry sleepers, the locked junction box where they keep the electricity. If you leave pennies on the rail the trains hammer them into long bronze tongues, the queen's face flattened to nothing.

Pan back and you're kneeling at the pond's edge because your brother says there are tadpoles. You reach into the soup of stems and slime, he shoves you and you're still screaming when you hit the surface.

Your mouth fills with water. Fear and loneliness will always taste like this. You run up the garden, sodden, trailing weed, shouting, *Dad . . . Dad . . . Dad . . .* And you can see him standing at the kitchen door, but he starts to evaporate as you reach the cracked patio, thinning in waves like Captain Kirk in the transporter room, that same high buzzing sound, and the door is empty, and the kitchen is empty, and the house is empty and you realise he's never coming back.

HAVE YOU NOT got anything else to read? asked Angela.

Yep, said Daisy, *but right now this is the book I would like to read if that's all right by you.*

There's no need to be sarcastic.

Ladies . . . said Alex, which would have escalated the row to flashpoint if they hadn't been interrupted by Benjy running down the carriage and pinballing off the seat backs. He'd been standing in the toilet when he remembered the werewolf from the Queen Victoria episode of *Doctor Who*. Eyes like black billiard balls, the heat of its breath on his neck. He squirrelled himself under Dad's arm and rubbed the silky cuff of Dad's special shirt against his upper lip. Dad said, *You all right, Captain?* and he said, *Yeh*, because he was now, so he took out his Natural History Museum notebook and the pen that wrote in eight colours and drew the zombies.

When he re-entered the world they were changing

trains at high speed, sprinting to another platform to catch a connecting train which left in two minutes. Halfway across the footbridge he remembered that he'd forgotten to pick up the metal thing. *What metal thing?* said Mum. *The metal thing*, he said, because he hadn't given it a name. It was a hinge from a brief-case and later on Mum would call it *a piece of rubbish* but he loved the strength of the spring and the smell it left on his fingers.

Dad said, *I'll get it* because when he was a child he kept a horse's tooth in a Golden Virginia tobacco tin, and Mum said, *For Christ's sake*. But Dad came back carrying the metal thing with seconds to spare and gave it to Benjy and said, *Guard it with your life*. And as they were pulling out of the station Benjy saw an old lady with long grey hair being arrested by two policemen in fluorescent yellow jackets. One of the policemen had a gun. Then there was another train travelling beside them at almost exactly the same speed and Benjy remembered the story about Albert Einstein doing a thought experiment, sitting on a tram in Vienna going at the speed of light and shining a torch straight ahead so the light just sat there like candyfloss.

You hate Richard because he swans around his spacious Georgian apartment on Moray Place four hundred miles away while you perch on that scuffed olive chair listening to Mum roar in the cage of her broken mind. *The nurses burn my hands. There was an air raid last night.* You hate him because he pays for all of it, the long lawn, the low-rent cabaret on Friday nights, *Magic Memories: The Stars of Yesteryear.* You hate him for marrying that woman who expected your children to eat lamb curry and forced you to stay in a hotel. You hate him for replacing her so efficiently, as if an event which destroyed other people's lives were merely one more medical procedure, the tumour sliced out, wound stitched and swabbed. You hate him because he is the prodigal son. *When will Richard come to see me? Do you know Richard? He's such a lovely boy.*

In spite of which, deep down, you like being the good child, the one who cares. Deep down you are still waiting for a definitive judgement in which you are finally raised above your relentlessly achieving brother, though the only person who could make that kind of judgement was drifting in and out of their final sleep, the mask misting and clearing, the low hiss of the cylinder under the bed. And then they were gone.

M6 SOUTHBOUND, THE sprawl of Birmingham finally behind them. Richard dropped a gear and eased the Mercedes round a Belgian chemical tanker. *Frankley Services 2 miles.* He imagined pulling over in the corner of the car park to watch Louisa sleeping, that spill of butter-coloured hair, the pink of her ear, the mystery of it, why a man was aroused by the sight of one woman and not another, something deep in the mid-brain like a sweet tooth or a fear of snakes. He looked in the rear-view mirror. Melissa was listening to her iPod. She gave him a deadpan comedy wave. He slid the Eliot Gardiner *Dido and Aeneas* into the CD player and turned up the volume.

MELISSA STARED OUT of the window and pictured herself in a film. She was walking across a cobbled square. Pigeons, cathedral. She was wearing the red leather jacket Dad had bought her in Madrid. Fifteen years old. She walked into that room, heads turned and suddenly she understood.

But they'd want her to be friends with the girl, wouldn't they, just because they were the same age. Like Mum wanted to be friends with some woman on the till in Tesco's because they were both forty-four. The girl could have made herself look all right but she hadn't got a clue. Maybe she was a lesbian. Seven days in the countryside with someone else's relatives. *It's a big thing for Richard.* Because keeping Richard happy was obviously their Function in Life. Right.

> *Shake the cloud from off your brow,*
> *Fate your wishes does allow;*
> *Empires growing,*
> *Pleasures flowing,*
> *Fortune smiles and so should you.*

Some idiot came past on a motorbike at Mach 4. Richard pictured a slick of spilt oil, sparks fantailing from the sliding tank, massive head trauma and the parents agreeing to the transplant of all the major organs so that some good might come of a short life so cheaply spent, though Sod's Law would doubtless apply and some poor bastard would spend the next thirty years emptying his catheter bag and wiping scrambled egg off his chin.

Dido and Aeneas. Groper Roper made them listen to it at school. *Pearls before swine.* Probably in prison by now. *Don't let him get you in the instrument cupboard.* It was a joke back then. *Interfering with children.* Looking back, though, it's Roper who feels like the victim, the taunts, those damp eyes, the kind of man who hanged himself in isolated woodland.

LOUISA WAS SLOWLY coming round. Classical music and the smell of the cardboard fir tree on the rear-view mirror. She was in the car with Richard, wasn't she. So often these days she seemed to hover between worlds, none of them wholly real. Her brothers, Carl and Dougie, worked in a car factory and lived six doors away from each other on the Blackthorn Estate. Not quite cars on bricks and fridges in the grass, not in their own gardens at least. When she visited they faked a pride in the sister who had bettered herself but what they really felt was disdain, and while she tried to return it she could feel the pull of a world in which you didn't have to think constantly of how others saw you. Craig had revelled in it. The two worlds thing, Jaguar outside the chip shop, donkey jacket at parents' evening.

Wales. She'd forgotten. God. She'd only met Richard's family once. *They liked you and you liked them.* Had they? Had she? She'd trumped them by wearing too much black. Benjamin, the little boy, was wearing a *Simpsons* T-shirt of all things. She overheard him asking his father what would happen to his grandmother's body *in the coming months.* And the way the girl sang the hymns. As if there might be something wrong with her.

RICHARD HAD BEEN seated next to Louisa at Tony Caborn's wedding, on what she correctly referred to as *the divorcees' table* in the corner of the marquee, presumably to quarantine the bad voodoo. Someone's discarded trophy wife, he thought. He introduced himself and she said, *Don't chat me up, OK?* She was visibly drunk. *I seem to be giving off some kind of vibes today.* He explained that he had no plans in that particular direction and she laughed, quite clearly at him rather than with him.

He turned and listened to a portly GP bemoaning the number of heroin users his practice was obliged to deal with, but his attention kept slipping to the conversation happening over his shoulder. Celebrity gossip and the shortcomings of Louisa's ex-husband, the wealthy builder. She was clearly not his kind of person, but the GP was his kind of person and was boring him to death. Later on he watched her stand and cross the dance floor, big hips but firm, something Nordic about her, comfortable in her body in a way that Jennifer had never been. *No plans in that particular direction.* He'd been a pompous arse. When she sat down he apologised for his earlier rudeness and she said, *Tell me about yourself,* and he realised how long it had been since someone had said this.

MUM WAS SMILING at Richard and doing the flirty thing where she hooked her hair behind her ear. It made Melissa think of them having sex, which disgusted her. They were in a traffic jam and Mika was singing 'Grace Kelly'. She took out a black biro and doodled a horse on the flyleaf of the Ian McEwan. How bizarre that your hand was part of your body, like one of those mechanical grabbers that picked up furry toys in a glass case at a fair. You could imagine it having a mind of its own and strangling you at night.

> *Mine with storms of care opprest*
> *Is taught to pity the distrest.*
> *Mean wretches' grief can touch,*
> *So soft, so sensible my breast,*
> *But ah! I fear, I pity his too much.*

He was thinking about that girl who'd turned up in casualty last week. Nikki Fallon? Hallam? Nine years old, jewel-green eyes and greasy blonde hair. He knew even before he'd done the X-rays. Something too malleable about her, too flat, one of those kids who had never been given the opportunity to disagree and had given up trying. Six old fractures and no hospital record. He went to tell the stepfather they'd be keeping her in. The man was slumped in one of the plastic chairs looking bored mostly, track-suit trousers and a dirty black T-shirt with the word BENCH on it. The man who'd abused her, or let others abuse her. He stank of cigarettes and after-shave. Richard wanted to knock him down and punch him and keep on punching him. *We need to talk.*

Yeh?

Richard's anger draining away. Because he was hardly more than a teenager. Too stupid to know he'd end up in prison. Sugar and boiling water thrown in his face on kitchen duty. *If you could come with me, please.*

MELISSA ROLLED UP the sleeves of Dad's lumber-jack shirt. Still, after all this time, the faintest smell of him. Plaster dust and Hugo Boss. He was an arse-hole, but, God, she looked at Richard sometimes, the racing bike, the way he did the crossword in pencil first. There were evenings when she wanted Dad to ride in off the plains, all dust and sweat and tumble-weed, kick open the saloon doors and stick some bullet holes in those fucking art books.

Land of hope and glory, sang Mika. *Mother of the free ride, I'm leaving Kansas, baby. God save the queen.*

HEREFORD, HOME OF the SAS. Richard could imagine doing that, given a Just War. Not the killing so much as the derring-do, like building dams when he was a boy, though it might be thrilling to kill another man if one were absolved in advance. Because people thought you wanted to help others whereas most of his colleagues loved the risk. That glint in Steven's eye when he moved to paediatrics. *They die quicker.*

Louisa had squeezed his hand at the graveside. Drizzle and a police helicopter overhead. That owner-less dog standing between the trees like some presiding spirit, his father's ghost, perhaps. He looked around the grave. These people. Louisa, Melissa, Angela and Dominic and their children, this was his family now. They had spent twenty years avoiding one another and he couldn't remember why.

MELISSA PRESSED PAUSE and gazed out of the window. Bright sun was falling on the road but there was rain far off, like someone had tried to rub out the horizon. That underwater glow. There'd be Scrabble, wouldn't there, a tatty box in some drawer, a pack of fifty-one playing cards, a pamphlet from a goat farm.

Real countryside now, the land buckled and rucked. *A sense sublime of something far more deeply interfused.* Blustery wind, trees dancing, flurries of orange leaves, a black plastic sack flapping on a gate. The road a series of bends and switchbacks. Richard driving too fast. Low pearly cloud. Turnastone. Upper Maescoed. Llanveynoe. They broached the top of a hill and the view was suddenly enormous. *Offa's Dyke,* said Richard. A dark ridge halfway up the sky. They made their way into the valley on a single-track road sunk between grassy banks like a bobsleigh run. Richard still driving too fast and Mum gripping the edge of the seat but not saying anything and . . . *Shit!* yelled Louisa, and *Fuck!* yelled Melissa, and the Mercedes skidded to a crunchy halt, but it was just a flock of sheep and an old man in a dirty jumper waving a stick.

TWO GLIDERS RIDE the freezing grey air that pours over the ridge, so low you could lean a ladder against the fuselage and climb up to talk to the pilot. Spits of horizontal rain, Hay Bluff, Lord Hereford's Knob. Heather and purple moor-grass and little craters of rippling peaty water. By the trig point a red kite weaves through the holes in the wind then glides into the valley, eyes scanning the ground for rats and rabbits.

This was shallow coastal waters once, before the great plates crushed and raised it. Limestone and millstone grit. The valleys gouged out by glaciers with their cargo of rubble. Upper Blaen, Firs Farm, Olchon Court. Roads and footpaths following the same routes they did in the Middle Ages. Everyone walking in the steps of those who walked before them. The Red House, a Romano-British farmstead abandoned, ruined, plundered for stone, built over, burnt and rebuilt. Tenant farmers, underlings of Marcher lords, a pregnant daughter hidden in the hills, a man who put a musket in his mouth in front of his wife and sprayed half his head across the kitchen wall, a drunken priest who lost the house in a bet over a horse race, or so they said, though *they* are long gone. Two brass spoons under the floorboards. A twenty-thousand-mark Reichsbanknote. Letters from Florence cross-written to save paper, now brown and frail and crumpled to pack a wall. *Brother, my Lungs are not Goode.* The sons of the family cut down at Flers-Courcelette and Morval. Two ageing sisters hanging on through the Second World War, one succumbing to cancer of the liver, the other shipped off to a nursing home in Builth Wells. Cream paint and stripped pine. The fire blanket in its red holster. *The Shentons – 22nd to 29th March – We saw a deer in the garden* . . . Framed watercolours of mallow and campion. Biodegradable washing-up liquid. A random selection of elderly, second-hand hardbacks. A pamphlet from a goat farm.

DOMINIC HAD ASKED for a people carrier but a Viking with an earring and a scar appeared in a metallic green Vauxhall Insignia. They had bags on their laps and the windows were steamed up and spattery with rain. Benjy was squashed between Mum and Daisy which he enjoyed because it made him feel safe and warm. He had been lonely at home because he wasn't allowed to play with Pavel for a week after the fight and getting blood all over Pavel's trousers, but he enjoyed being on holiday, not least because you were allowed pudding every night. He had never spoken to Uncle Richard but he knew that he was a radiologist who put tubes into people's groins and pushed them up into their brains to clear blockages like chimney sweeps did and this was a glorious idea. An articulated lorry came past riding a wave of spray and for a few seconds the car seemed to be underwater, so he imagined being in the shark submarine from *Red Rackham's Treasure*.

ALEX TOTTED UP how much the holiday was going to cost him. Two missed shifts at the video shop, two dog walks. A hundred and twenty-three quid down. But the hills would be good. Lots of kids thought he was boring. He couldn't give a fuck. If you didn't earn money you were screwed. He'd get through college without a loan at this rate. He rubbed his forehead. Tightness behind his left eye and that sour taste in the back of his throat. Fifteen minutes and the pain would arrive, flurries of lime-green snow sweeping across his field of vision. He opened the window a crack and breathed in the cold air. He needed darkness. He needed quiet.

Oi, said Dad, but when he turned he saw the expression on Alex's face. *Do we need to pull over?*

Alex shook his head.

Ten minutes, OK?

They turned off the main road and suddenly they were out of the rain, the world cleaned and glittering. They roller-coastered over a little summit and Offa's Dyke hove into view, a gash of gold along the ridge, as if the sky had been ripped open and the light from beyond was pouring through.

Holy shit, Batman, said Benjy, and no one told him off.

BEESWAX AND FRESH linen. Louisa stood in the centre of the bedroom. A hum from deep underground, just on the limit of hearing, a chill in the air. Hairs stood up on the back of her neck. Someone had suffered in this room. She'd felt it since childhood, in this house, in that corridor. Then Craig bought Danes Barn and she couldn't bear to be in there for more than five minutes. He told her she was being ridiculous. A week later she heard about the little boy who'd hidden in the chest freezer.

MELISSA WALKED DOWN the cold tiles of the hall and into the bright rectangle of the day. She took her earphones out. That silence, like a noise all by itself, with all these other noises inside it, grass rubbing together, a dog yapping far off. She dried the rain from the bench with a tea towel and sat down with *Enduring Love*, but she couldn't hang on to the words because she'd never spent more than five consecutive days in the countryside before. Kellmore in Year 11. Ziplines and Bacardi Breezers. Kasha's epileptic fit in the showers. There really was absolutely nothing to do here. She had two joints at the bottom of her bag but she'd have to smoke them up there with the sheep. Richard stoned. Jesus. Imagine that. *Goodness, I don't think I've realised how amazing this Mozart Piano Concerto is. We haven't got any more biscuits, have we?* But it *was* beautiful, when you thought about it, this huge green bowl, clouds changing shape as they moved, the smell of woodsmoke. A banana-yellow caterpillar reared up like a tiny question mark on the arm of the bench. She was about to flick it away when she imagined it having a name in a children's book, but suddenly there was a green taxi bumping through the gate and Alex and his little brother spilt from the door like clowns from a circus car.

... STUNNING VIEWS *of the Olchon Valley* ... *Grade 2 listed* ... *sympathetically restored* ... *a second bathroom added* ... *large private garden* ... *shrubbery, mature trees* ... *drowning hazard* ... *mixer taps* ... *a tumble dryer* ... *no TV reception* ... *£1,200 per week* ... *all reasonable breakages* ... *American Express* ... *the septic tank* ...

DOMINIC HELPED THE driver unload while Benjy retrieved the briefcase hinge from a crumb-filled recess. Richard hugged Angela with one arm, his mug of tea at arm's length. Post-rain sparkle and the dog still yapping far off. Daisy shook Richard's hand and unnerved him slightly by saying, *It's good to see you again*, as if she was a colleague, so he turned to Benjamin. *And how are you doing, young man?*

Melissa held Alex's eye for two seconds and he forgot briefly about the nausea. *Unzipping*. Maybe normal service really was being suspended. But Melissa saw how much he wanted her and how naïve he was and the week seemed no longer empty. She walked slowly towards the front door, his gaze like sun on her back. *Bitch*, thought Angela, but Alex could see the first flurries of green snow and had to get to the bathroom. She had that glossy, thoroughbred look, thought Daisy.

Hair you shook in slow motion. Leader of some icy little coven at school. But being fashionable and popular were shallow things which passed away. Daisy had to remember that. Shallow people were people nevertheless, and equally deserving of love.

The Vauxhall Insignia did a four-point turn and drove off scraping its manifold on the ruts and there was silence in the garden so that the red kite, looking down, saw only a large square of mown grass tilted towards the opposite side of the valley and, sitting confidently at its geometric centre, a house, stately and severe and adamantly not a farmhouse. Tall sash windows, grey stone laid in long, thin blocks, a house where Eliot or Austen might have lodged a vicar and his fierce teetotal sisters. A drystone wall ran round the boundary of the property, broken by two gates, one for walkers, one for carriages, both of ornate cast iron now thick with rust. A weather vane in the shape of a running fox. There were rhododendrons and a shallow ornamental pond thick with frogspawn. There was the skull of a horse in the woodshed.

ALEX SLUICED HIS mouth under the cold tap and felt his way back across the landing with his eyes closed. He lowered himself onto the bed, put the pillow over his head to cut out light and noise and curled into a ball.

*

ANGELA HAD BEEN trapped by Louisa in the kitchen with a glass of red wine. That expensive mildew taste. *Melissa's vegetarian. I'd happily give up meat as well, but Richard is a bit of a caveman.*

Why did she dislike this woman? The cream roll-neck, the way she held the measuring jug up to the light, for example, as if it were a syringe and a life hung in the balance. Onions fizzed in the pan. She thought about Carl Butcher killing that cat last term. *They were swinging it against a wall, Miss.* She'd recognised the policeman from Cycle Proficiency. Carl's hard little face. All those boys, they knew the world didn't want them, bad behaviour their only way of making some small mark. *But people eat cows.* Most intelligent thing he'd said all year.

God alone knows how she's going to survive here, said Louisa. *A hundred miles from the nearest branch of Jack Wills.*

A YELLOW TRACTOR and the sun setting over Offa's Dyke, tumble-down barns with corrugated iron roofs, the hill so steep Daisy felt as if she were looking out of a plane window, no noise but the wind. She could have reached out and picked that tractor up between her thumb and forefinger. This was Eden. It wasn't a fairy story, it was happening right now. This was the place we were banished from. A bird of prey floated up the valley until it was swallowed by the green distance. The fizzy tingle of vertigo in the arches of her feet. The centuries would swallow us like the sky swallowing that bird. She and Melissa had passed one another on the landing earlier. She said hello but Melissa just stared at her as they moved around one another, spaghetti western-style, everything in slo-mo.

A red Volvo was zigzagging slowly up from Longtown, vanishing and reappearing with the kinks in the road. Down the hill she could see Benjy in the walled garden doing Ninja moves with a stick. *Oof . . .! Yah . . .!* No one could see her out here, no one could judge her. She looked at herself in the mirror and saw the animal that she was trapped inside, that grew and fed and wanted. She wished above all else to look ordinary so that people's eyes just slid over her. Because Mum was wrong. It wasn't about believing this or that, it wasn't about good and evil and right and wrong, it was about finding the strength to bear the discomfort that came with being in the world.

Clouds scrolled high up. She couldn't get Melissa out of her head. Something magnetic about her, the possibility of a softness inside, the challenge of peeling back those layers.

BEERS IN HAND, Dominic and Richard stood looking over the garden wall, gentlemen on the foredeck, a calm, green sea beyond. *Angela tells me you've got yourself a job in a bookshop.* Dominic had been unemployed for nine months, apparently. *Bespoke or chain?*

Waterstone's, said Dominic. *Best job I've ever done, to be honest.* He looked up. No contrails because of the volcanic ash. The way the fields stopped half-way up the hill and gave way to gorse and bracken and scree, that darkness where the summit met the sky, Mordor and The Shire within fifty yards of one another.

Really? asked Richard. But how did one lose one's job if one was self-employed? Surely one simply had more or less work coming in. A talented musician, too. Richard remembered visiting their house some years back and Dominic entertaining the children with a jazz version of 'Twinkle, Twinkle, Little Star' and the *Blue Peter* theme tune in the style of Beethoven. But he made his living composing music for adverts, washing powder and chocolate bars. Richard found it hard to comprehend anyone embarking upon a career without aiming for the top. Which applied to Angela as well, though she was a woman with children, which was different. And now he'd let it all slip through his fingers.

Amazing place, said Dominic, rotating slowly to take in the whole panorama.

You're welcome, said Richard.

*

BENJY PAUSES BY the hall table and leafs idly through the *Guardian*. He is fascinated by newspapers. Sometimes he stumbles on things that terrify him, things he wishes he could undiscover. Rape, suicide bombers. But the pull of adult secrets is too strong. *Four thousand square miles of oil drifting from the Deepwater Horizon rig . . . Thirty people killed by bombs in Mogadishu . . . Fifty tonnes of litter found in a whale's stomach . . .* He has been thinking a lot about death lately. Carly's dad from school who had a heart attack aged forty-three. Granny's funeral. There was a woman on the television who had anal cancer.

He puts the paper down and begins exploring the house, entering every room in turn and making a mental map of escape routes and places where enemies might be hiding. He can't go into the bedroom because Alex is having a migraine so he heads downstairs in search of a knife to make a spear but Auntie Louisa is in the kitchen so he goes outside and finds a big stick in the log shed. He hacks off a zombie's head and blood sprays from the neck stump and the head lies on the ground shouting in German until it is crushed under one of his horse's hooves.

ALEX SLID HIS legs over the edge of the bed and sat up slowly, shirt soaked in sweat. His head felt bruised and the colour of everything was off-key, as if he were trapped inside a film from the sixties. At least

Melissa hadn't seen him like this. When it happened at school he had to go and lie down in the sickbay. He tried to pass it off as an aggressive adversary he overcame by being tough and stoical, but he knew that some kids thought it was a spazzy thing like epilepsy or really thick glasses. He rubbed his face. He could smell onion frying downstairs and hear Benjy battling imaginary foes outside. *Oof . . .! Yah . . .!*

MELISSA POPPED OPEN the clattery little Rotring tin. Pencils, putty rubber, scalpel. She sharpened a 3B, letting the curly shavings fall into the wicker bin, then paused for a few seconds, finding a little place of stillness before starting to draw the flowers. Art didn't count at school because it didn't get you into law or banking or medicine. It was just a fluffy thing stuck to the side of Design and Technology, a free A level for kids who could do it, like a second language, but she loved charcoal and really good gouache, she loved rolling sticky black ink on to a lino plate and heaving on the big black arm of the Cope press, the quiet and those big white walls.

DAISY WALKED INTO the living room and found Alex sitting on the sofa drinking a pint of iced water and staring at the empty fireplace. *How are you doing?*

Top of the world. He held up his glass in a fake toast. The ice jiggled and clinked.

Always these stilted conversations, like strangers at a cocktail party. *I went for a walk up the hill. It's, like, Alex World up there.*

He seemed confused for a moment, as if trying to remember where he was. *Yeh, I guess so.*

A couple of years back he'd been a puppy, unable to sit down for a whole meal, falling off the trampoline and using his plastered arm as a baseball bat. They'd played chase and snakes and ladders and hide and seek with Benjy and watched TV lying on top of one another like sleeping lions. He seemed like another species now, so unimpressed by life. Dad's breakdown hardly touched him. She'd read one of his history essays once, something about the economic problems in Germany before the Second World War and the Jews being used as scapegoats, and she was amazed to realise that there was a person in there who thought and felt. *What do you reckon to Melissa?*

She's all right.

He was talking rubbish. He obviously fancied her because boys couldn't think about anything else. She wanted to laugh and grab his hair, start one of the play fights they used to have, but there was a force-field, and the rules had changed. She reached out to touch the back of his neck but stopped a couple of centimetres short. *See you at supper.*

You will indeed.

*

RICHARD OPENED THE squeaky iron door of the stove. Ash flakes rose and settled on the knees of his trousers. He scrunched a newspaper from the big basket. *PORT-AU-PRINCE DEVASTATED*. A grainy photo of a small boy being pulled from the rubble. No one really cared until there were cute children suffering. All those little blonde girls with leukaemia while black teenagers in London were being stabbed every day of the week. He flirted with the possibility of a firelighter but it seemed unmanly, so he built a tepee of kindling around the crumpled paper. An image of the Sharne girl passed through his mind. *She rowed for Upper Thames.* Think of something else. He struck a match. Swan Vesta. The way they lay in the box reminded him of the stacked trunks by Thorpe sawmill. The paper caught and the flame was an orange banner in a gale. He closed the door and opened the vent. Air roared in. His knees hurt. He needed to do more exercise. He imagined making love with Louisa later on, the cleanness of her skin after a shower, the cocoa butter body wash that made her taste like cake.

THEY'RE HIDING IN *the trees*, said Daisy, *with bows and arrows. And we've got the secret plans.*

Secret plans for what?

She peeled a lump of moss off the edge of the bench. *For a moon rocket.*

This is boring, said Benjy.

She thought about the men with bows and arrows. They were really here, weren't they, once upon a time. And mammoths and ladies in crinolines and Spitfires overhead. Places remained and time flowed through them like wind through the grass. Right now. This was the future turning into the past. One thing becoming another thing. Like a flame on the end of a match. Wood turning into smoke. If only we could burn brighter. A barn roaring in the night.

ANGELA LOOKED OUT of the bedroom window. Dominic and Richard chatting at the edge of the garden, the way men did, beer in one hand, the other hand thrust into a trouser pocket, both staring straight ahead. She wondered what they were talking about and what they were avoiding talking about. Forty-seven years old and she still felt a fifteen-year-old girl's anger at the younger brother who had teamed up with Mum and frozen her out after Dad died. She took the Dairy Milk from the bottom of her case, tore back the paper and the purple foil, snapped off the top row of chunks and put them into her mouth. That nursery rush. Mum and Richard had visited Dad in hospital the day before he died. Angela wasn't allowed to go and she was haunted for months afterwards by a recurring nightmare in which they had conspired somehow to cause his death. Someone banged a large pan downstairs and shouted, *Dinner*, like they were guests in a country house. Flunkeys and silver salvers. She'd better go and join the fray.

DAISY, PLEASE. ANGELA reached out to grab her sleeve. *Not now.* But Dominic was standing in the way and she couldn't reach.

What were you going to say? asked Richard.

Grace, replied Daisy. *I was going to say grace.*

The room snapped into focus, wine bottles green as boiled sweets, galleons on the table mats. Melissa let her mouth hang open comically.

Fire away, said Richard, who was accustomed to situations where other people felt uncomfortable.

Oh Lord . . . People drifted through life with their eyes closed. You had to wake them up. *We thank You for this food, we thank You for this family and we ask You to provide for those who have no food, and to watch over those who have no family.*

Amen and a-women, said Benjy.

Excellent. Richard rubbed his hands together, Melissa said, *Fucking Nora*, under her breath and the scrape of chairs on the flagstones was like a brace of firecrackers. Louisa lifted the red enamelled lid of the big pot and steam spilt upwards.

Alex looked over at Daisy and gave her a thumbs-up. *Nice one, sister.*

Dominic poured two centimetres of wine into Benjy's wine glass.

Is this place not wonderful? asked Richard, widening his arms to indicate the house, the valley, the countryside, perhaps life itself.

Louisa was frightened of talking to Daisy. She didn't know any proper Christians, but Daisy said, *I love that sweater*, and suddenly it wasn't so bad after all.

Richard raised his glass. *To us*, and everyone raised their glasses. *To us*. Benjy drank his wine in one gulp.

Melissa saw Daisy and Mum laughing together. She wanted to force them apart, but there was something steely about the girl. She wouldn't back down easily, would she?

Alex couldn't stop looking at Melissa. That terrible yearning in his stomach. He was imagining her in the shower, foam in her pubes.

Angela looked at Richard and thought, *We have nothing in common, nothing*, but Richard eased back into his chair. *You remember that dead squirrel we found on the roundabout in the park?* He swung the wine around his glass like a man in a bad advert for wine. *We thought it was a miracle.*

How do you remember this stuff? But why had she forgotten? That was the real question.

He closed his eyes as if running a slideshow in his mind's eye. *The tapestry cushion covers. God Almighty. Cats, roses, angels . . .*

She felt obscurely violated. This was her past too, but he had stolen it and made it his own.

Fuck. Melissa leapt to her feet, tomato sauce all over her trousers. *You little shit.*

Hey, hey, hey. Louisa raised her hands but Melissa swept out.

I'm sorry, said Benjy. *I'm really really sorry.* He was crying.

Come here, little man. Dominic hugged him. *You didn't mean to do it.*

But Alex felt a weight lift. No more sexual inter-ference messing with his head.

Teenage girls, said Richard to the table in general, his tone neutral, as if he were opening the subject up for discussion.

Yes, she remembered now. The dead squirrel. So perfect, the tiny claws, as if it had simply lain down to sleep.

Can I have some more wine? asked Benjy.

This tastes good.

Morrisons in Ross-on-Wye, amazingly.

Nine weeks we had the builders in.

He went to Eton.

Ouch.

There's plasters in my toilet bag.

Twenty stone at least.

You got blood in the Parmesan.

She had a fractured skull.

Fifty press-ups.

Apple crumble.

A quarter of a million people.
Brandy? Cigars?
Dizzee with a double E . . .
And then the Hoover blew up. Literally blew up.
Sit down. I'll do the washing-up.
I'm stuffed.
Bedtime, young man.
Up in them thar hills.
Goodnight, Benjy.
Daisy, will you read to him?
Teeth. Remember what the lady said.
Night, Benjy.
Night-night.

SHE SAT ON the floor between the bedside table and the wall. Laughter downstairs. She pushed the point of the scalpel into the palm of her hand but she couldn't puncture the skin. She was a coward. She would never amount to anything. That fuckwit little boy. She should walk off into the night and get hypothermia and end up in hospital. That would teach them a lesson. God. Friday night. Megan and Cally would be tanking up on vodka and Red Bull before hitting the ice rink. The dizzy spin of the room and Lady Gaga on repeat, Henry and his mates having races and getting chucked out, pineapple fritters at the Chinky afterwards. Christ, she was hungry.

*

PAOLO'S FATHER DIED *and he went back to Italy.* Dominic handed Louisa a wet plate. *And I discovered that I wasn't very good at selling myself.* He tipped the dirty water out of the bowl and refilled it from the hot tap. *I was in a band at college. I thought I'd be famous. Sounds ridiculous now. We were into Pink Floyd. Everyone else was listening to The Clash.*

I was listening to Michael Jackson. She held up her hands, begging forgiveness.

Eventually you realise you're ordinary.

Melissa appeared at the door and Louisa pressed the start button on the microwave. Dominic saw that there was a bowl of apple crumble already in there, waiting. While it turned and hummed in the little window Louisa laid her hand on Melissa's forearm for three or four seconds as if performing some kind of low-grade spiritual healing. She took a pot of yoghurt from the fridge, a spoon from the drawer and laid them neatly beside one another on the worktop. *Thanks,* said Melissa quietly and for a fraction of a second Dominic saw the little girl under the veneer.

THE TREES WERE *thinning up ahead and Joseph could see gashes of sunlight between the trunks. He picked up speed and ten seconds later he stumbled out from between the pines into a space so big and bright that he stood on the little beach, stunned, trying to take it in* (Daisy shifted position to make her back more comfortable). *They were looking at a lake, rippled and silver under the grey sky. They had been living underground for so long it felt like the ocean. Mellor opened the map. 'We've arrived,' he said.*

'What do you mean?' asked Joseph.

(Benjy's eyelids were getting heavy.)

Mellor pointed out across the water. 'The house is out there.'

Joseph's heart sank. 'The map has to be wrong.'

'Ssshh . . .' Mellor put his finger to his lips.

In the distance Joseph could hear the faint barking of dogs. The Smoke Men were coming.

(Benjy closed his eyes and turned over.)

Mellor stuffed the map hurriedly into his rucksack. 'Quick. Take off your boots.'

RICHARD PULLED HIS shirt over his head. *She has to learn some manners.*

She's sixteen.

I don't care how old she is.

You can't force children to do anything.

So you let them do exactly what they want?

Richard, you are not her father. Sorry. I didn't mean that . . .

No, I'm sorry. He shook his head like a dog coming out of water. *It's the Sharne case. It's getting to me.*

You did nothing wrong.

Being innocent is not always enough.

Come here.

But he wouldn't come. *I'm going outside to clear my head.*

DOMINIC STARED AT the black grid of the uncurtained window. If only he could fly away. How had he not seen the danger when Amy came into the shop that day? Blonde eyebrows, albino almost. They'd talked in the playground six years before. Two boys a couple of years above Daisy. She lingered at the till and he wondered if she was flirting but it had been so long that he found it hard to be certain. Then she mentioned her address in a way that was clearly an invitation which could be ignored without embarrassment and he dreamt that night of her long pale body with a vividness he had not felt since he was twenty. They slept together three weeks later in the middle of the afternoon, something he and Angela had never done, and this in itself was thrilling. She made a great deal of noise so that he wondered, briefly, if she were in actual pain. They lay afterwards looking up at the big Japanese paper lantern turning in the dusty curtained glow and Amy said, *Thank you, kind sir.* He turned onto his side and ran his fingers over her hip bones and her little breasts and into deep dints above her collarbones and realised there was a secret door in the house where he had been trapped for so long.

*

ANGELA WAS TWO hundred miles and thirty-five years away, trying to conjure the hallway of the house where she'd grown up, the newel post they called The Pineapple, the china tramp that lay on the carpet smashed one morning as if a ghost had brushed past in the night, the Oscar Peterson Trio on the gramophone. Dominic climbed into bed and the bounce of the mattress woke her briefly. She listened to the silence and thought of Benjy and felt the old fear. Was he still breathing? A cracked wooden beam ran across the ceiling, splinted with a rusty iron spar. She was slipping away a little now. Sherbet Dabs and Slade singing 'Cum on Feel the Noize'. Briefly she saw Karen sitting in the darkness somewhere further up the hill, looking down on the sleeping house, like a rabbit or an owl. Then she let go.

DAISY OPENED THE book and put the Monet postcard to one side.

I sat down beside her, and presently she moved uneasily. At the same moment there came a sort of dull flapping or buffeting at the window. I went over to it softly, and peeped out by the corner of the blind. There was a full moonlight, and I could see that the noise was made by a great bat, which wheeled around, doubtless attracted by the light, although so dim, and every now and again struck the window with its wings.

*

FINGERNAIL MOON. THE Bay of Rainbows. The Sea of Tranquillity. Richard had never really got the space thing. It worried him, the possibility that his imagination wasn't strong enough to get past the earth's atmosphere. Neil Armstrong's heart rate staying under seventy during take-off. *All brave men are slightly stupid*. He and Mohan had sat opposite one another at the table by the window. He can see it as clear as day. Mohan was eating a container of M&S salad with a white plastic fork. *It could be an abscess*. Of course he should have put it in the report, that was precisely why he had tracked Mohan down, to make sure. Now the girl was in a wheelchair and Mohan was pretending the conversation never happened. Everyone knew the man was a shit, sleeping with two nurses and his poor bloody wife without a clue, which counted for nothing in a court of law, of course, just gossip and hearsay. The way the lawyer stared at him during that meeting. He half expected his eyelids to slide in from the side. Bloody hell, it was freezing out here.

WITH A LITTLE grunt, Alex came messily into the cone of toilet tissue in his right hand then leant back against the door, breathing heavily. That sudden disinterest, pictures of Melissa naked blowing away like mist. He wiped the splash from the wooden floor with the toe of his sock. He was thinking about canoeing on Llyn Gwynant. Then he was thinking about how quiet the house was and whether anyone had heard him. Richard's shaving brush glared from the window sill. He imagined it containing a little camera. Richard sitting at the dining table replaying the grainy footage, saying, *Angela, I think you should see this*. He dropped the tissue into the toilet bowl, pulled the flush and smelt his fingers. Seasidey. Nice.

You run your hand along the bumpy, magnolia wall. Paint over paint over plaster over stone, smooth, like the flank of a horse. Something alive in the fabric of the house. Earlier today, in Café Ritazza at Southport, Richard had put his hands behind his head and stretched out as if he owned the place. Polo shirt, TAG Heuer watch. A young mum was staring from a nearby table, pink tracksuit, scraped-back hair. He looked through her like she was furniture. But Melissa does have to learn some manners, and maybe you haven't been strict enough. You remember yourself at fourteen. The Hanwell flat. You and Penny standing on the outside of the balcony rail, seven floors up, one Sunday afternoon, leaning over that woozy drop, hearts pounding and the scary tickle in the back of your knees. Dogs in the park, the traffic on the ring road, a scale model of the world. You whoop as loud as you can and your voice bounces off the block opposite. There's a little crowd gathering now. Someone shouts, *Jump*. You look around and it occurs to you that this isn't real, this is only a memory, that you could let go and topple into that great windy nothing and it wouldn't matter. What frightens you is that for a couple of seconds you can't remember where the present is and how to get back there.

THE CLICK OF the Mercedes cooling. A barn owl on top of a telegraph pole, eyeballs so big they rub against one another as they revolve. Bats slice the air above the garden. Limestone freakishly white under the moon. The sheep lie beside an old bath, still gathered against the wolves which haven't hunted them for two hundred years. The deep quiet under the human hum. Bootes, Hercules, Draco. Eight thousand man-made objects orbiting the earth. Dead satellites and space junk. The asteroid belt. Puck, Miranda, Oberon. To every moon a fairy story. The Mars Rover squatting near the Husband Hills. The Huygens probe beside a methane lake on Titan. The Kuiper belt. Comets and Centaurs. The Scattered Disc. The Oort Cloud. The Local Bubble. Barnard's Star. The utter cold warmed only by starlight.

RICHARD MADE HIS way down the dark stairs. He couldn't use the bathroom on the landing because of the tangled pipes under the sink. Tubing, plumbing, large-bore wiring. *Phobia* never quite described it. *A discrete period of intense fear or discomfort in which at*

least 4 of the following 13 symptoms develop abruptly . . .
The four in his case being a choking sensation, feelings of unreality, abdominal distress and a fear of going
insane. He couldn't use Car Park E at work because it
meant walking past the ducts at the back of the heating block. Last year he'd been standing on the Circle
Line platform at Edgware Road en route to a confer-
ence in Reading. The brickwork on the far side of the
tracks invisible behind a great rolling wave of sooty
cables. He came round with a gash on his head
looking up at a ring of people who seemed to have
gathered to watch a fight in the playground.

He unbuttoned his pyjama fly and aimed just left
of the water to minimise the noise. He should get his
prostate checked. The floor was cobbled and cold and
the walls smelt of damp but the sink down here was
enclosed in a wooden cabinet and the ribbed white
shower flex was single and therefore benign. He flushed
the toilet and washed his hands. Bed.

Breathe

SHE LEAVES THE institute, takes the Red Line to Davis and walks back home. She stands in the empty house and feels sick in the pit of her stomach. And then it comes to her. There is nothing keeping her here any more. She can go, just go, leave everything behind. She packs two bags, leaves the keys in the mailbox and takes a taxi to Logan where the next BA departure has a last-minute seat in club class going for a song. An omen maybe, if she believed in such things.

She nurses an espresso in Starbucks and imagines the sour little woman from Fernandez & Charles standing in the living room wondering what the fuck to do with the exercise ball and the Balinese shadow puppet and the armchairs from Crate and Barrel. On the table to her right two Mormons sit side by side, strapping farm boys in black suits, Elders Thorsted and Bell, the names on their badges as big as signs on office doors. On her left an ebony-skinned man in an intricately embroidered white djellaba is reading a book called *The New Financial Order*. There are four messages on her phone. She pops the back off, drags the SIM card out with her fingernail and flips both phone and card into the waste bin.

Her flight comes up and she boards. A glass of complimentary champagne, pull back from the stand, a short taxi, those big turbines kick in and she is lifted from the surface of the earth. An hour later she is eating corn-fed chicken, wild-mushroom sauce and baby fennel as night streams past outside. She falls into a deep sleep where she dreams not the old dream of crashing and burning but a new dream of cruising forever in the radiation and the hard light and the deep cold and when she wakes they are banking over the reservoirs of Hertfordshire on their descent into Heathrow.

The train clatters north from Euston. The deep chime of the familiar. Chained dogs in scrapyards, level crossings, countryside like a postcard, all her history lessons written on the landscape, Maundy money and 'Ring a Ring o' Roses'. She should have called ahead. At least this way she can creep up on the place from downwind, see what it looks like when it doesn't know she's watching then turn round and move on if that's what feels right.

She gets out of the taxi and stands on Grace Road,

looking across the big grass triangle that sits at the centre of the estate, tower blocks on two sides, a row of shops on the third, a playground in the centre, the kind of place which must have looked fantastic as an architectural model before it got built and real human beings moved in.

There is a Nisa Local, there is a chip shop called the Frying Squad. Between the two is the Bernie Cavell Advice Centre. Two boys are doing BMX stunts on the big rock in the centre of the pedestrian precinct which they used to call the Meteorite. She turns left and walks past Franklin Tower, the smell from the bins still rancid in the December chill.

17 Watts Road. A shattered slate lies on the path in front of the house. It's mid-afternoon but behind the dirty glass all the curtains are closed. The bell isn't working. She raps the letter box, waits then raps it again but gets no reply. Something passes through her. Despair or relief, she can't tell. She crouches and looks through the slot. It is dark and cold in the hall-way, some faint urinous scent.

'Mum . . .!' Briefly she is nine again, wearing a green duffel coat and those crappy socks which slid down under your heel inside your wellingtons. She raps the letter box for a third time. 'Hello . . . ?'

She checks that no one is watching then breaks the glass with her elbow, the way it's done in films. She reaches through the broken pane and feels a shiver of fear that someone or something is going to grab her hand from inside. She slips off the safety chain and turns the latch.

The smell is stronger in the hallway, damp, unclean. There is a fallen pagoda of post on the phone table and grey fluff packs out the angle between the carpet and the skirting board. Here and there wallpaper has come away from the damp plaster. Can she hear something moving upstairs or is it her imagination?

'Mum . . . ?'

The only light in the living room is a thin blade of weak sun that cuts between the curtains. She stops on the threshold. A body is lying on the floor. It is too small to be her mother, the clothes too ragged. She has never seen a corpse before. To her surprise what she feels, mostly, is anger, that someone has been squatting in her mother's house and that she now has to sort out the resulting mess. She covers her nose and mouth with her sleeve, walks around the room and crouches for a closer look. The woman is older than she expects. She lies on a stained mattress, knotted grey hair, dirty nails, a soiled blue cardigan and a long skirt in heavy green corduroy. Only when she recognises the skirt does she realise that she is looking at her mother.

'Oh Jesus.'

She wants to run away, to pretend that she was never here, that this never happened. But she has to inform the police. She has to ring her sister. She crouches, waiting for her pulse to slow and the dizziness to pass. As she is getting to her feet, however, her mother's eyes spring open like the wooden eyes of a puppet.

'Holy fuck!' She falls backwards, catching her foot and cracking her head against the fire surround.

'Who are you?' says her mother, panicking, eyes wide.

She can't speak.

'I haven't got anything worth stealing.' Her mother stops and narrows her eyes. 'Do I know you?'

She has to call an ambulance but her mind has gone blank and she can't remember the emergency number in the UK.

'It's Carol, isn't it?' Her mother grips the arm of the sofa and lifts herself slowly onto her knees. 'You've changed your hair.' She gathers herself and stands up. 'You're meant to be in America.'

'I thought you were dead.'

'I was asleep.'

'You were on the floor.' The back of her head is throbbing.

'I was on the mattress.'

'It's the middle of the day.'

'I have trouble with the stairs.'

Dust lies thick on every horizontal surface. The framed Constable poster is propped beneath the rectangle of unbleached wallpaper where it used to hang, the glass cracked across the middle.

'I thought you hated us,' says her mother. 'I thought you were going to stay away forever.'

This is the room where she and Robyn ate tomato soup and toast fingers in front of *Magpie* and *Ace of Wands*. This was where they played Mousetrap and threw a sheet over the coffee table to make a cave.

'What happened?'

'I was asleep.'

'To the house. To you.'

'Your father died.'

'And then what?'

There was a lime tree just beyond the back fence. It filled the side window and when the wind gusted all the leaves flipped and changed colour like a shoal of fish. The window is now covered with a sheet of plywood.

'How did you get in?' says her mother.

'Mum, when did you last have a bath?'

'I spent forty-three years looking after your father.'

'I can actually smell you.'

'Enough housework to last a lifetime.'

'Does Robyn know about all this?'

'Then I no longer had to keep him happy. Not that I ever succeeded in keeping your father happy.'

'She never said anything.'

'I prefer not to go out. Everyone is so fat. They have electric signs that tell you when the next bus is coming. I should make you a cup of tea.' And with that she is gone, off to make God alone knows what bacterial concoction.

Carol picks the papier mâché giraffe from the windowsill and blows the dust off. She can still feel the dry warmth of Miss Calloway's hands wrapped around her own as they shaped the coat-hanger skeleton with the red pliers, coffee and biscuits on her breath from the staffroom at break. 'Come on, squeeze.'

SHE ASKS THE woman behind the till in the Nisa for the number of a local taxi firm and rings from a call box. Sitting on a bench waiting for the cab she remembers the street party they held to celebrate the wedding of Charles and Diana in July of 1981, everyone getting drunk and dancing to Kim Wilde and the Specials on a crappy PA in the bus shelter. *This town . . . is coming like a ghost town.*

There were trestle tables down the centre of Maillard Road but no timetable beyond a rendition of 'God Save the Queen' and a half-hearted speech by a local councillor which was rapidly drowned out by catcalls. The atmosphere became rowdier as the day went on, the older people dispersing around nightfall when the air of carnival turned sinister. She remembers a woman sitting on the grass and weeping openly. She remembers Yamin's terrifying older brother having sex with Tracey Hollywood on the roundabout while his mates whooped and spun it as fast as they could. She remembers the Sheehan twins firing rockets across the field until the police arrived, then starting up again when they left. For months afterwards you would find little plastic Union Jacks and lager cans and serviettes bearing pictures of the royal couple wedged into the nettles at the edge of the football pitch and stuck behind the chicken-wire fence around Leadbitter's Bakery.

She remembers how Helen Weller's brother jumped from a seventh-floor balcony in Cavendish Tower one Christmas while high on mushrooms, equipped only with a Spider-Man bed sheet. She remembers Cacharel and strawberry Nesquik and Boney M singing 'Ra Ra Rasputin'. She remembers how her father would stand at the front window staring out on all of this and say, *Look on my works, ye mighty, and despair.* Only many years later did she realise that he hadn't made the phrase up himself, though whether he was pretending to be Shelley or Ozymandias she still doesn't know.

ROBYN IS TAKING wet washing from the machine. The dryer churns and rumbles. Through the half-opened concertina doors Carol can see the children watching *Futurama*. Fergal, Clare and Libby. She can never remember which girl is which. There are crayon pictures in cheap clip frames. There are five tennis rackets and a space hopper and a dead rubber plant and two cats. The clutter makes Carol feel ill. 'Jesus, Robyn, how did you let it happen?'

'I didn't let anything happen.'

'I'm pretty certain she'd wet herself.'

'So you got her undressed and put her into the bath and helped her into some clean clothes?'

Robyn has put on two stone at least. She seems fuzzier, less distinct.

'Six years. Shit, Carol. Why didn't you tell us you were coming?'

'She's my mother, too.'

'Christmas cards, the odd email.' Robyn slams the washing-machine door and hefts the laundry basket onto a chair.

'Let's not do this.'

'Do what? Draw attention to the fact that you waltzed off into the sunset?'

'Why didn't you tell me?'

'You never asked.'

'Asked what? "Has Mum gone crazy?"'

'She's not crazy and you never asked about anything.'

The argument is unexpectedly satisfying, like getting a ruler under a plaster and scratching the itchy, unwashed flesh. 'This is not about scoring points. This is about our mother who is sleeping on the floor in a house full of shit.'

'You didn't come back when Dad was dying.'

'We were in Minnesota. We were in the middle of nowhere. I didn't get your message till we got back to Boston. You know that.'

'You didn't come to his funeral.'

Carol knows she should let it go. Her life has exceeded Robyn's in so many ways that her sister deserves this small moral victory, but it niggles, because the story is true. She remembers it so clearly. There were eagles above the lake and chipmunks skittering over the roof of the cabin. Every room smelt of cedar. Down at the lakeside a red boat was roped to a wooden quay. She can still hear the putter of the outboard and the slap of waves against the aluminium hull. 'How often does she get out?'

'I pop in on Tuesdays and Thursdays after work and do her a Sainsbury's shop on Saturday morning.'

'So she never goes out?'

'I make sure she doesn't starve to death.' Robyn looks at her for a long moment. 'How's Aysha, Carol?'

How can Robyn tell? This X-ray vision, her ability to home in on a weakness. Is it being a mother, spending your life servicing other people's needs? 'Aysha's fine. As far as I know.'

Robyn nods but doesn't offer any sisterly consolation. 'Secondaries in his lungs and bone marrow. They sewed him up and sent him to the hospice.'

'I know.'

'No, Carol. You don't know.' Robyn picks out three pairs of socks and drapes them over the radiator below the window. 'He collapsed in the bathroom, his trousers round his ankles.'

'You don't need to do this.'

'The doctor was amazed he'd managed to keep it hidden for so long.' She takes a deep breath. 'I've always pictured you sitting in the corner of the kitchen with your hands over your ears while the phone rings and rings and rings.' The dining table is covered in half-made Christmas cards, glitter glue and safety scissors and cardboard Santas. 'Sometimes people need you,' says Robyn. 'It might be inconvenient and unpleasant but you just do it.'

SHE BOOKS INTO the Premier Inn and eats a substandard lasagne. Her body is still on Eastern Standard Time so she sits in her tiny room and tries to read the Sarah Waters she bought at the airport but finds herself thinking instead about her father's last days, that short steep slope from diagnosis to death.

Lake Toba in Sumatra used to be a volcano. When it erupted 70,000 years ago the planet was plunged into winter for a decade and human beings nearly died out. The meteorite that killed the dinosaurs was only six miles across. The flu epidemic at the end of the First World War killed 5 per cent of the world's population. Some fathers told their little girls about

Goldilocks and Jack and the Beanstalk, but what use were stories? These were facts. We were hanging on by the skin of our teeth and there was nowhere else to go in spite of the messages you might have picked up from *Star Trek* and *Doctor Who*. She remembers Robyn weeping and running from the room.

He left school at sixteen then spent thirty years building and decorating. Damp rot, loft conversions, engineered wood flooring. He liked poetry that rhymed and novels with plots and pop science with no maths. He hated politicians and refused to watch television. He said, 'Your mother and your sister believe the world's problems could be solved if people were polite to one another.'

Which is why he didn't want her to leave, of course. He was terrified that she'd get far enough away to look back and see how small he was, a bullying, bar-room philosopher not brave enough to go back to college for fear he might get into an argument with people who knew more than he did.

Pancreatic cancer at fifty-seven. 'All that anger. It turns on you in the end,' was Aysha's posthumous diagnosis and for once Carol was tempted to agree with what she'd normally dismiss as hippy bullshit.

Sometimes, on the edge of sleep, when worlds overlap, she slips back forty years and sees the sun-shaped, bronze-effect wall clock over the fireplace and feels the warmth of brushed cotton pyjamas straight from the airing cupboard and her heart goes over a humpbacked bridge. Then she remembers the smell of fried food and the small-mindedness and her desperation to be gone.

She presses her forehead against the cold glass of the hotel window and looks down into the car park where rain is pouring through cones of orange light below the street lamps. She is back in one of the distant outposts of the empire, roughnecks and strange gods and the trade routes petering out.

She abandoned her mother. That hideous house. She has to make amends somehow.

She climbs into bed and floats for eight hours in a great darkness lit every so often by bright little dreams in which Aysha looms large. The dimples at the base of her spine, the oniony sweat which Carol hated then found intoxicating then hated once more, the way she held Carol's wrists a little too tight when they were making love.

They met at an alumni fund-raiser about which she remembered very little apart from the short, muscular woman with four silver rings in the rim of her ear and a tight white T-shirt who materialised in front of her with a tray of canapés and a scowl, after which all other details of the evening were burned away.

She had the air of someone walking coolly away from an explosion, all shoulder roll and flames in the background. A brief marriage to the alcoholic Tyler.

RIP, thank God. Three years on the USS *John C. Stennis* – seaman recruit E-1, culinary specialist, honourable discharge. A mother who spoke in actual tongues at a Baptist church in Oklahoma. Somewhere in the background, the Choctaw Trail of Tears, the Irish potato famine and the slave ports of Senegambia if Aysha's account of her heritage was to be believed, which it probably wasn't, though she had the hardscrabble mongrel look. And if the powers that be had tried to wipe out your history you probably deserved to rewrite some of it yourself. She was self-educated, with more enthusiasm than focus. Evening classes in philosophy, Dan Brown and Andrea Dworkin actually touching on the bookshelf, a box set of Carl Sagan's *Cosmos*.

Two months later they were in the Hotel de la Bretonnerie in the Marais, Aysha's first time outside the States unprotected by fighter aircraft. Aysha had gone sufficiently native to swap Marlboro for Gitanes but she was sticking to the Diet Coke. They were sitting outside a little cafe near the Musée Carnavalet.

Aysha said, 'Thank you.'

'You don't owe me anything,' said Carol.

'Hey, lover.' Aysha held her eye. 'Loosen up.'

THE FOLLOWING MORNING she hires a Renault Clio and drives to the house via B&Q and Sainsbury's. Her mother is awake but doesn't recognise Carol at first and seems to have forgotten their meeting of the previous day, but perhaps the back foot is a good place for her to be on this particular morning. Carol dumps her suitcases in the hall, turns the heating on and bleeds the radiators with the little brass key which, thirty years on, still lies in the basket on top of the fridge. The stinky hiss of the long-trapped air, the oily water clanking and gurgling its way up through the house.

'What are you doing?' asks her mother.

'Making you a little warmer.'

She rings a glazier for the broken window.

'I've changed my mind,' says her mother. 'I don't like you being here.'

'Trust me.' She can't bring herself to touch the dirty cardigan. 'It's going to be OK.'

The noises are coming from the built-in cupboard in the bedroom she and Robyn once shared. Scratching, cooing. She shuts the landing door, opens the windows and arms herself with a broom. When she pulls the handle back they explode into the room, filling the air with wings and claws and machine-gun clatter. She covers her face but one of them still gashes her neck in passing. She swings the broom. 'Fuck . . .!' They bang against the dirty glass. One finds the open window, then another. She hits a third and it spins on the ground, its wing broken. She throws a pillow over it, stamps on the pillow till it stops moving then pushes pillow and bird out of the window into the garden.

She boards up the hole in the wall where they have scratched their way in, takes two dead birds to the bin outside then stands in the silence and the fresh air, waiting for the adrenalin to ebb.

Back inside, the radiators are hot and the house is drying out, clicking and creaking like a galleon adjusting to a new wind. A damp, jungle smell hangs in the air. Plaster, paper, wood, steam, fungus.

'This is my home,' her mother says. 'You cannot do this.'

'You'll get an infection,' says Carol. 'You'll get hypothermia. You'll have a fall. And I don't want to explain to a doctor why I did nothing to stop it happening.'

She puts the curtains into the washing machine. She drags a damp mattress down the stairs and out onto the front lawn. Half the slats of the bed are broken so she takes it apart and dumps it on top of the mattress. She has momentum now. The carpet is mossy and green near the external wall so she pulls it up and cuts it into squares with blunt scissors. The underlay is powdery and makes her cough and coats her sweaty hands with a brown film. She levers up the wooden tack strips using a claw hammer. She adds everything to the growing pile outside. She sweeps and hoovers till the bare boards are clean, then takes the curtains out of the washing machine and hangs them over the banisters to dry.

She sponges the surface of the dining table and they eat lunch together on it, a steak-and-ale puff-pastry pie and a microwaved bag of pre-cut vegetables. Her mother's anger has melted away. The lunchtime TV news is on in the background. '*Who Wants to Be This* and *Get Me Out of That*,' says her mother. 'All those women with plastic faces. Terrorists and paedophiles. We called it "interfering with children". Frank, who worked in Everley's, the shoe shop, he was one. I'm certain of that.' She stares into her plate for a long time. 'A woman drowned herself in the canal last month. That little bridge on Jerusalem Street? Jackie Bolton. It was in the paper. You were at school with her daughter. Milly I think her name was.' Carol has no memory of a Milly. 'I'd go out more if I still lived in the countryside. There was a flagpole by the pond in the centre of the village. They put it up for the coronation. Your Uncle Jack climbed all the way to the top and fell off and broke his collarbone.'

Carol must have heard the story twenty times. It is oddly comforting.

Her mother leans over and takes Carol's hand. 'I thought I might never see you again.'

Her skin has a sticky patina, like an old leather glove. 'We need to get you into the bath.'

She is compliant until halfway up the stairs when she looks through the banisters and sees the uncarpeted boards in the bedroom. 'You're selling the house.'

'Don't be ridiculous.' Carol laughs. 'It's not mine to sell.' She doesn't say how little she thinks it would fetch, in this state, on this road.

'That's why Robyn hates you being here.'

'Jesus Christ, Mum.' Carol is surprised by how angry she feels. 'I could be in California, I could be working, but I'm stuck here on a shitty estate in the middle of nowhere trying to turn this dump back into a house before it kills you.'

'You thieving little . . .' She slaps Carol's face with her free hand, loses her footing and for a second she is falling backwards down the stairs until Carol grabs her and hauls her upright.

'Shit.' Carol's heart is hammering. In her mind's eye her mother is lying folded and broken by the front door. She loosens her grip on the bony wrist. 'Mum . . . ?'

Her mother doesn't reply. She is suddenly blank and distant. Carol should take her downstairs and sit her on the sofa but she might not get this chance again. She puts her hands on her mother's arms and guides her gently up the last few steps.

She removes her mother's shoes and socks. She peels off the soiled blue cardigan and unzips the dirty green corduroy skirt. Both are heavily stained and patched with compacted food. She takes off her mother's blouse, unclips the grey bra and kicks all the clothing into the corner of the room. Her mother's skin is busy with blotches and lesions in winey purples and toffee browns, the soft machinery of veins and tendons visible under the skin where it is stretched thin around her neck, at her elbows, above her breasts. The smell is rich and heady. Carol tries to imagine that she is dealing with an animal. She takes off her mother's slip and knickers, perches her on the rim of the bath, lifts her legs in one by one then lowers her mother into the hot, soapy water. She flips the corduroy skirt over the pile of discarded clothing so she can't see the brown streaks on the knickers then sits on the toilet seat. She'll bin them later. 'Hey. We did it.'

Her mother is silent for a long time. Then she says, 'Mum filled a tin bath once a week. Dad got it first, then Delia, then me.' She is staring at something way beyond the wall of dirty white tiles. 'There was a sampler over the dining table. Gran made it when she was a girl. "I saw an angel come down from heaven, having the key of the bottomless pit and a great chain in his hand." The angel locks the dragon in a pit for a thousand years. After that he must be "loosed a little season".' She looks at Carol and smiles for the first time since she arrived. 'Are you going to wash my hair?'

*

CAROL MAKES THEM each a mug of coffee. Now that her mother is clean the room looks even more squalid. Old birthday cards, a china bulldog with a missing leg, mould in the ceiling corners, one of those houses cleared out post-mortem by operatives in boiler suits and paper masks.

They hear the click and twist of a key in the front door. Robyn is in the hallway. 'There's a pile of stuff outside.'

'I know.'

She steps into the living room and looks around. 'What the hell are you doing, Carol?'

'Something you should have done a long time ago.'

'You can't just ride in here like the fucking cavalry.' Robyn silently mouths the word *fucking*.

'What's going on?' says her mother.

'There were pigeons in the bedroom,' says Carol.

'How long are you staying?' asks Robyn. 'A week? Two weeks?'

'Carol?' says her mother. 'What are you two arguing about?'

'Jesus,' says Robyn. 'Fucking up your life doesn't mean you can take over someone else's instead.' This time she says the word out loud.

'Carol gave me a bath,' says her mother.

'Did you hurt her?'

It is too stupid a question to answer.

'Aysha rang me.' Robyn holds her eye for a long

time. 'Sounds like you left a trail of destruction in your wake.'

Carol assumes at first that she has misheard. Aysha talking to Robyn is inconceivable.

'She wanted to check you hadn't killed yourself or been sectioned. I'm giving you the highlights. Some of the other stuff you probably don't want to hear.'

'How did she get your number?' asks Carol.

'I presumed you'd given it to her in case of emergencies. Her being your partner.'

There is something barbed about the word *partner* but Carol isn't sure who or what is being mocked.

'We'd have come to the wedding,' says Robyn. 'I like weddings. I like America.'

'What are you both talking about?' says her mother.

'I'm taking Mum out for dinner,' says Carol, though the thought had not occurred to her until that moment.

Robyn stands close enough so that their mother can't hear. 'She's not a toy, Carol. You can't do this. You just can't.'

Then she is gone.

'THERE'S TOO MUCH going on.'

Carol looks around the half-empty Pizza Express.

'Too much noise,' says her mother. 'Too many people.'

There is a low buzz of conversation, some cutlery-clatter. Rod Stewart is singing 'Ruby Tuesday' faintly from the speaker above their heads. She rubs her mother's arm. 'I'm here and you're safe.' She wonders if her sister's apparent care disguises something more sinister, her mother's supposed fear of the outside world a fiction Robyn uses to keep her in the house. But her mother is becoming increasingly agitated and when the food arrives she says, 'I really don't feel very well.'

'Come on. That pasta looks fantastic. When was the last time you had a treat?'

Her mother stands up, knocking a water glass to the floor where it shatters. Carol grabs her mother's arm but there is no way she can hang on to it without making the scene look ugly. She lets her mother go, puts thirty pounds on the table, runs for the door and finds her sitting at a bus stop, crying and saying, 'Why did you bring me here? I want to go home.'

When they pull up outside the house her mother says, 'I don't want you to come inside.'

She could throw her bags into the car and go, to London, to Edinburgh, to anywhere in the world, leaving her mother to live the narrow and grubby life to which she has become addicted. But the phrase *anywhere in the world* gives her that queasy shiver she's been experiencing on and off since Aysha left, the sudden conviction that everything is fake, the fear that she could step through any of these doors and find herself on some blasted heath with night coming down, the world nothing more than a load of plywood flats collapsing behind her. 'I'm staying. I don't want to leave you on your own.'

'One night.'

SHE LIES IN a sleeping bag on the blow-up mattress, orange street light bleeding through the cheap curtains, sirens in the distance. It is thirty years since she last slept in this room. For a brief moment those intervening years seem like nothing more than a vivid daydream of escape. She'd got into Cambridge to read Natural Sciences, driven in equal parts by a fascination with the subject and a desperation to put as much distance as possible between herself and this place. A doctorate at Imperial and a postdoc in Adelaide. Jobs in Heidelberg, Stockholm . . . working her way slowly up the ladder towards Full Professor. Four years max in any one country had been the rule. Out of restlessness, partly, though it was true that she ruffled feathers, and ruffled feathers were easier to live with if they were on a continent where you no longer lived.

She is not a team player, so she has been told on more than one occasion, usually by men who were quite happy to stab someone else in the back so long as the victim wasn't a member of whatever unspoken brotherhood they all belonged to. But she has run successful groups and the grants have followed her and in the end the world doesn't give a damn about a few cuts and bruises if it gets a firmer grip on ageing or diabetes, or a clearer picture of how one cell swallowed another and ended up flying to the moon.

Boston was her fourth position as a group leader, running a lab working on the mammalian target of rapamycin complex. Two years in, however, Paul Bachman became the institute's new director and everything started to turn sour. He brought with him a blank cheque from Khalid bin Mahfouz and instead of supporting the existing faculty went on a global hiring spree. Enter the Golden Boys who deigned sometimes to attend faculty meetings or listen to sub-stellar visiting academics but only as a favour. Paul himself had a house in Bar Harbor and a yacht called *Emmeline* and a younger wife with a breathtakingly low IQ. Feeling at home wasn't Carol's strong suit but under the new dispensation she started to feel like a junior member of the golf club.

In other circumstances she'd have put out feelers, quietly letting colleagues elsewhere know that she had itchy feet. But she'd just met Aysha and, to her astonishment, they were sharing a house, so she knuckled down and put up with the Cinderella treatment.

Eighteen months later, out of nowhere, Aysha said she wanted to get married. Because that's what loving someone meant, apparently, gathering your families and friends from the four corners of the globe, dressing up, making public vows, getting a signed certificate. Like you hadn't proved it already by putting up with the subterfuge and the vilification. Carol didn't understand. The straight world shut you out for two thousand years, the door opened a crack and you were meant to run in and curl up by the fire like grateful dogs. What was wrong with being an outsider? Why this desperate urge to belong to a world which had rejected you?

A year later she and Aysha were no longer sharing a house because . . . the truth was that she was still not entirely sure. It was the kind of puzzle there was no point trying to solve, the kind of puzzle you didn't have to solve if you sloughed off all the human mess every few years, trimmed your life down to a few suitcases and headed off for a new skyline, new food, a new language.

Two months of panic and claustrophobia came to an end when Daniel Seghatchian from Berkeley threw her a lifeline, asking if she'd come over and give a chalk talk, meet the faculty, meet the postdocs. Just getting off the plane in California was a relief. Space and sunlight and opportunity. The Q&As were tough but they felt like the respectful aggression meted out to a worthy opponent and by the end of three days the position seemed pretty much in the bag.

She wonders now if the whole thing had been a trap of some kind. Is that possible? Or was it merely her blindness to the allegiances and loyalties and lines of communication upon which others built whole careers?

Her first morning back in Boston she was summoned by Paul who asked what she had against the institute. He didn't explain how he'd heard the news so quickly. Only later did she realise that he wasn't asking her what they could do to persuade her to stay. He was giving her enough rope to hang herself. He listened to her diatribe and if she had been a little less exhausted by three days of non-stop thinking she might have asked herself why he seemed untroubled, pleased even. He waited for her to finish then leaned back in his chair and said, 'We'll miss you, Carol.' And only walking away from his office, thinking back to this obvious lie, did she wonder what unseen wheels were turning.

Three days later she got a call from Daniel Seghatchian saying that there was a problem with funding.

'Three minutes of grovelling,' Suzanne said, sitting in her office that lunchtime. 'You won't really mean it. Everyone else will know you don't really mean it. Paul will know you don't really mean it. Or, shit, maybe you will mean it. Either way, you go through a little ceremony of obeisance. Kneel before the king. Ask for a pardon. He loves all that stuff.'

Why had that seemed such an impossible thing to do?

After talking to Suzanne she went to the regular meeting with her three postdocs working on the PKCα project. They were in the room that looked onto the little quadrangle with the faux-Japanese garden. Minimal concrete benches, rectangular pond, lilac and callery pear, wind roughening the surface of the water. She was finding it hard to concentrate on what was being said. She was thinking about the last walk she took on Head of the Meadow Beach in Provincetown with Aysha. She was thinking about the humpbacks out on the Stellwagen Bank. Three thousand miles a year, permanent night at forty fathoms, cruising like barrage balloons above the undersea ranges.

Suddenly the room was full of water. Shafts of sunlight hung like white needles from the surface high above her head. Darkness under her feet, darkness all around. Ivan was talking but his voice was tinny and unreal as if he were on a radio link from a long way away. 'Breathe,' he was saying. 'You have to breathe.' But she couldn't breathe because if she opened her mouth the water would rush in and flood her lungs.

FINALLY, DESPITE THESE churning thoughts she passes into shallow sleep until she comes round just after three on the tail end of a scratchy, anxious dream in which she hears someone entering the house. Unable to sleep without reassuring herself she gets out of bed and goes downstairs to find the living room empty and her mother gone. She runs into the street but it is silent and still. She puts her shoes on, checks the garden then jogs once round the estate's central triangle calling, 'Mum ... ? Mum ... ?' as if her mother is a lost dog.

A pack of hooded teenage boys cycle past, slowing to examine her, then sweeping silently onward. She comes to a halt at the junction of Eddar and Grace Roads where the taxi dropped her off forty-eight hours ago. A scatter of lights still burn in Cavendish and Franklin Towers like the open doors in two black Advent calendars. The cherry-red wing tip of a plane flashes slowly across the dirty, starless sky. A dog is barking somewhere. *Yap ... yap ... yap ...* It is a couple of degrees above freezing, not a good night for an old woman to be outside.

She returns to the house and as she puts the key into the lock she remembers her mother's story of Jackie Bolton drowning herself in the canal. She puts the key back into her pocket and starts to run. Harrow Road, Eliza Road. A milk float buzzes and tinkles to a halt on Greener Crescent. She is flying, the surface of the world millpond-smooth while everyone sleeps. A fox trots casually out of a gateway and watches her, unfazed. Jerusalem Road. She stops on

the little bridge and looks up and down the oily rib-
bon of stagnant water. Nothing. 'Shitting shit.' She
walks down the steps onto the gravelled towpath and
sees her mother standing on the little strip of weeds
and rubble on the far side of the canal. It is like seeing a ghost. The blankness of her mother's stare, the
black water separating them.

'Don't move.'

She runs down the towpath to a decayed cantilever
footbridge. She heaves on the blocky, counterweighted
arm and it comes free of the ground, the span bumping down onto the far side of the little bottleneck in
the stream. She steps gingerly across the mossy slats,
squeezes round a fence of corrugated iron and kicks
aside an angry swirl of barbed wire.

She comes to a halt a little way away, not wanting
to wake her mother abruptly. 'Mum . . . ?'

Her mother turns and narrows her eyes. 'You've
always hated me.'

'Mum, it's Carol.'

'I know exactly who you are.' It is a voice Carol has
not heard before. 'But I look at you and all I see is your
father.'

Her mother is tiny and cold and she is wearing a
thick skirt and a heavy jumper which would become
rapidly waterlogged. How long would it take? And
who would know? The thought passes through her
mind and is gone.

Her mother's glare holds firm for several seconds then her face crumples and she begins to cry. Carol takes her hand. 'Let's get you home.'

THE REGISTRAR SAYS they are keeping her in overnight. Carol leaves a message for Robyn. On the ward her mother is unconscious so she drinks a styrofoam cup of bitter coffee in the hospital cafe, doing the quick crossword in *The Times* to distract herself from something gathering at the edge of her imagination. Whales cruising in the dark, right now, just round the corner of the world. The sheer size of the ocean, crashed planes and sunken ships lost until the earth's end. Serpentine vents where everything began. Images from a magazine article she'd read years ago of the *Trieste* six miles down in the Mariana Trench, steel crying under the pressure, a ton of water on every postage stamp of metal.

Robyn sits down opposite her.

'She walked out of the house in the middle of the night.'

'Sweet Jesus, Carol. You've only been here two days.'

She stops herself saying, 'It wasn't my fault,' because it probably is, isn't it? She can see that now.

'You're just like Dad. You think everyone else is an idiot.'

'She's going to be OK.'

'Really?'

'She had a shock. She's exhausted.'

'You can't just decide how you want things to be, Carol. That's not how the world works.' She sounds more exasperated than angry, as if Carol is a tiresome child. 'Some people's minds are very fragile.'

THE DOCTOR IS plump and keen and seems more like a schoolboy prodigy than a medical professional. 'Dr Ahluwalia.' He shakes their hands in turn. 'I will try to be quick and painless.' He takes a pencil from his pocket and asks Carol's mother if she knows what it is.

She looks at Carol and Robyn as if she suspects the doctor of being out of his mind.

'Humour me,' says Dr Ahluwalia.

'It's a pencil,' says her mother.

'That is excellent.' He repockets the pencil. 'I'm going to say three words. I want you to repeat them after me and to remember them.'

'OK.'

'Apple. Car. Fork.'

'Apple. Car. Fork.'

'Seven times nine?'

'My goodness, I was never any good at mental arithmetic.'

'Fair enough,' says Dr Ahluwalia, laughing gently along with her.

Carol can see her mother warming to this man and is suddenly worried that she can't see the trap which is being laid for her. Her mother tells the doctor the date and her address. 'But you'll have to ask my daughter for the phone number. I don't ring myself very often.'

Dr Ahluwalia asks her mother if she can repeat the phrase, 'Do as you would be done by.'

'Mrs Doasyouwouldbedoneby.' Her mother smiles, the way she smiled in the bath. 'I haven't heard that name for a long time.' She drifts away with the memory.

'Mum . . . ?'

Dr Ahluwalia glances at Carol and raises an eyebrow, the mildest of rebukes.

'Mrs Doasyouwouldbedoneby,' says her mother, 'and Mrs Bedonebyasyoudid.'

Dr Ahluwalia asks her mother if she can make up a sentence. 'About anything.'

'It's from *The Water Babies*,' says her mother. 'We read it at school. Ellie is very well-to-do and Tom is a chimney sweep.' She closes her eyes. '"Meanwhile, do you learn your lessons, and thank God that you have plenty of cold water to wash in; and wash in it too, like a true Englishman."' She is happy, the bright pupil who had pleased a favourite teacher.

'Excellent.' Dr Ahluwalia takes a notepad from his pocket and draws a pentagon on the top sheet. He tears it off and hands it to her mother. Every page is inscribed with the words *Wellbutrin – First Line Treatment of Depression*. 'I wonder if you could copy that shape for me.'

She seems unaware of how little resemblance her battered star bears to its original but Dr Ahluwalia says, 'Lovely,' using the same bright tone. 'Now, I wonder if you can tell me those three objects whose names I asked you to remember.'

Her mother closes her eyes for a second time and says, slowly and confidently, 'Fire . . . clock . . . candle . . .'

THE EMPTY HOUSE scares her. Carol tries reading but her eyes keep sliding off the page. She needs something trashy and moreish on the television but she can't bring herself to sit in a room surrounded by so much crap so she starts cleaning and tidying and it is the sedative of physical work that finally comforts her. She ties the old newspapers in bundles and puts them outside the front door. She stands the mattress against a radiator in the hall to air and dry. She puts the cushion covers on a wool cycle and dusts and hoovers. She cleans the windows. She rehangs the Constable poster and puts a new bulb into the standard lamp.

She finishes her work long after midnight then goes upstairs and falls into a long blank sleep which is broken by a phone call from Robyn at ten the following morning saying that she and John will bring their mother home from hospital later in the day.

She digs her trainers from the bottom of her suitcase and puts on the rest of her running gear. She drives out to Henshall, parks by the Bellmakers Arms and runs out of the village onto the old sheep road where their father sometimes took them to fly the kite when they were little. It's good to be outside under a big sky in clear, bright air away from that godforsaken estate, the effort and the rhythm hammering her thoughts into something small and simple. Twenty minutes later she is standing in the centre of the stone circle, just like she and Robyn did when they were girls, hoping desperately for a sign of some kind. And this time something happens. It may be nothing more than a dimming in the light, but she feels suddenly exposed and vulnerable. It's not real, she knows that, just some trait selected thousands of years ago, the memory of being prey coded into the genome, but she runs back fast, a sense of something malign at her heels the whole way, and she doesn't feel safe until she gets into the car and turns the radio on.

SHE PACES THE living room, a knot tightening in the base of her stomach. She dreads her mother coming home in need of constant care and Robyn saying,

'You've made your bed, now lie in it.' She dreads her mother coming home in full possession of her senses and ordering her to leave. She dreads the car not turning up at all and afternoon turning to evening and evening turning to night. And then there is no more time to think because her mother is standing in the doorway saying, 'This is not my house.'

'Don't be silly.' Carol shows her the papier mâché giraffe. 'Look.'

'This is definitely someone else's house.' She seems very calm for someone in such a disconcerting situation.

Robyn steps round her mother and into the room. 'What did you do, Carol?'

'I cleaned and tidied.'

'This is her home, Carol. For fuck's sake.'

'You can't make me stay here,' says her mother.

'Mum . . .' Carol blocks her way. 'Look at the curtains. You must remember the curtains. Look at the sideboard. Look at the picture.'

'Let me go.' Her mother pushes her aside and runs.

Robyn says, 'Are you happy now?'

Carol can't think of an answer. She's lost confidence in the rightness of her actions and opinions. She feels seasick.

'I hope you have nightmares about this,' says Robyn, then she turns and leaves.

*

SHE DRIVES TO the off-licence and returns with a bottle of vodka and a half-litre of tonic water. She pours herself a big glass and sits in front of the television, scrolling through the channels in search of programmes from her childhood. She finds *The Waltons*. She finds *Gunsmoke*. She watches for two hours then rings Robyn.

'I don't think I want to talk to you.'

'I'm sorry.'

'No you're not, Carol. I don't think you know the meaning of the word.'

It strikes her that this might be true. 'Where's Mum?'

'Back on the ward. They still had a bed, thank God.'

'And what's going to happen to her?'

'You mean, what am I going to do now that you've smashed her life to pieces?'

Was it really possible to destroy someone's life by giving them a bath and cleaning their house? Could a life really be held together by dirt and disorder?

'Have you been drinking?'

She can't think of a reply. Perhaps she really is drunk. The line goes dead.

SHE RETURNS TO the television. *Columbo, Friends*. It is dark outside now and being drunk isn't having the anaesthetic effect she hoped. She watches a documentary about the jungles of Madagascar. She sleeps and wakes and sleeps and wakes and somewhere in between the two states it becomes clear how much she loved Aysha, how much she still loves her, and how it is the strength of those feelings which terrifies her. Then she sleeps and wakes again and it is no longer clear.

She comes round with a grinding headache and sour sunlight pouring through the gap in the curtains. She rifles through the kitchen drawers and finds some antique ibuprofen and washes down two tablets with tonic water. She remembers how the cleaning and tidying of yesterday calmed her mind. So she takes a collection of planks from the broken bed in front of the house and stacks them in the centre of the lawn at the back, then breaks the rusty padlock from the shed door with a chunk of paving stone. Inside, everything is exactly as her father left it, concertinas of clay pots, jars of nails and screws, balls of twine, envelopes of seeds (Stupice early vine tomatoes, Lisse de Meaux carrots . . .), a fork, a spade . . . The lighter fuel is sitting in a little yellow can on the top shelf. She sprinkles it on the pyramid of wood and sets it alight. When it is blazing she drags the mattress outside and folds it over the flames. Through a gap in the fence a tiny woman in a pink shalwar kameez and headscarf is watching her, but when Carol catches her eye she melts away.

There were twins there once, two scrawny boys with some developmental problem. Donny and Cameron, was it? Their mother worked in the Co-op.

The mattress catches. The smell is tart and chemical, the smoke thick and black. She takes the sofa cushions outside and adds them to the pyre. Then, one by one, the dining chairs. She hasn't been this close to big unguarded flames since she was a child. She's forgotten how thrilling it is. And out of nowhere she remembers. It was the one public-spirited thing her father did, building and watching over the estate's bonfire in the run-up to Guy Fawkes Night. Perhaps being an outsider was a part of it. Ferrymen, rat catchers and executioners, intermediaries between here and the other place. Or perhaps her father was simply scary enough to stop the more wayward kids starting the celebrations with a can of petrol in mid-October. She remembers how he drove out to the woods behind the car plant and brought back a bag of earth from the mouth of a fox's den then built the fire round it so that the scent would keep hedgehogs and cats and mice from making a home inside. It is a tenderness she can't remember him ever showing to another human being.

She goes back inside the house. Someone is knocking at the front door. Then they are knocking on the front window. Shaved head, Arsenal shirt. 'You're a fucking headcase, you are. I'm calling the council.'

She burns the poster, the glass shattering in the heat. She hasn't sweated like this in a long time. It feels good. She burns the ornaments and the knick-knacks and the bundles of newspapers. She stares into the heart of the fire as light drains slowly from the sky.

It starts to rain so she goes indoors. She rips up the carpet and the tack strips just like she's done upstairs. She cuts the carpet into squares and throws them into the garden. The black wreckage of the bonfire steams and smokes. She sweeps and hoovers the floorboards. The TV and the curtains are the only remaining objects in the room.

She is too tired to do any more work but she is frightened of silence. She makes herself a large vodka and tonic. She sits with her back against the wall and scrolls through the channels until she finds a band of white noise in the mid-eighties. She turns the volume up so that the room is filled with grey light and white noise. She lies down and closes her eyes.

THE PHONE IS ringing. She has no idea what time it is. She lies motionless just inside the border of sleep, like a small animal in long grass waiting for the circling hawk to ride a thermal to some new pasture. The phone stops.

She dreams that she is a little girl standing in the stone circle. She dreams that she is flying over mountains. She dreams that she is looking down into a pit containing a dragon. She hears someone saying, over and over, 'The fire, the clock and the candle,' but she doesn't know what it means.

'CAROL . . . ?'

She opens her eyes and sees that dawn is coming up.

'Carol . . . ?'

The TV screen fizzes on the far side of the room. Her hip and shoulder hurt where they were pressed against the hard, wooden floor. Why does the person calling her name not come through to the living room to find her? She gets slowly to her feet, flexing her stiff joints. She squats for a few seconds until the room stops swaying.

'Carol . . . ?'

She thinks about slipping out the back door but it seems important that she doesn't run away. Has she perhaps run away on a previous occasion with dire consequences? She can't remember. Steadying herself with a hand on the wall she steps into the hall but sees only two blank rectangles of frosted daylight hanging in the gloom.

'Carol . . . ?'

She turns. An old man is standing in the kitchen doorway. He is wearing pyjamas and there is a battered yellow tank strapped to an old-fashioned porter's trolley at his side. He presses a mask to his face and takes a long, hissy breath. 'It's good to see you.' His voice is raspy and small. She half recognises him and this reassures her somewhat but she has no idea where she has seen him before and doesn't want to appear foolish by asking.

He presses the mask to his face, takes a second hissy breath, drapes the rubber tube over the handle of the trolley and rolls it past her towards the front door. He stops on the mat and holds out his hand. 'Come.'

She is nervous of going with this man but the thought of staying here on her own is worse. She takes his hand. He opens the door and Carol sees, not the houses on Watts Road but long grass and foliage shifting in a breeze. He takes another breath through his mask and bumps the trolley wheels over the threshold. They step into cold, clear winter light. He leads her slowly down a cinder path into a stand of trees. She can feel how weak he is and how much effort he is making not to let this show. She moves closer so that she can share more of his weight without this being obvious. He takes nine steps then stops to breathe through the mask, then eight more steps, then another breath.

They are among the trees now, dancing submarine light and coins of sun like fish around a reef. The trees are birch, mostly, bark curling off the creamy flesh like wallpaper in a long-abandoned house. She wonders what will happen when the oxygen runs out. The tank is clearly very old, the yellow paint so chipped that it has become a map of a ragged imaginary coastline.

They enter a large clearing. It is hard to see precisely how big the clearing is because it is occupied almost entirely by a great mound of logs and branches and sticks, woven like a laid winter hedge in places and in other places simply heaped up higgledy-piggledy. The whole edifice rises steeply in front of them, curving away so that it is impossible to tell whether the summit is fifty or a hundred and fifty feet high.

The man squeezes her hand and moves gingerly forward again. They enter a narrow corridor in the structure, like the tunnel leading to the burial chamber of a pyramid. He is her father, she remembers now. There is something not right about him being here but she doesn't know what. She is tired, her head hurts and she slept badly. Perhaps that is the problem.

Her eyes become accustomed to the low light and she can make out the monumental fretwork of beams and branches which surrounds them. Here and there shafts of sunlight cut across the bark-brown gloaming. Little twigs crunch underfoot and the poorly oiled wheels of her father's trolley squeak. There is dust in the air and the smell of fox.

Now they are standing in the central chamber, a rough half-dome of interwoven sticks some eight or

nine feet high, the tonnage above their heads sup-
ported by a central column as thick and straight as a
telegraph pole.

'Carol . . . ?'

The voice is muffled and distant. It is a woman's
voice and it is coming from outside. Only now does
she realise that it was not her father who was calling
her name when she woke. Was she wrong to follow
him? He takes a little yellow can from his pocket,
unscrews the top and pours the contents all over his
pyjamas. The smell is potent and familiar but Carol
can't give it a name and there is not enough light to
read the writing on the label.

'Carol . . . ?' The voice is more urgent now.

Her father puts the can back into his pocket and
lifts something from the other pocket. Only when he
spins the flint does she realise what it is. The flame
leaps the gap between his hand and his pyjama jacket,
spreading quickly across his torso, climbing upwards
over his face and digging its long violet fingers into
his hair.

'Carol . . . ? For God's sake . . .'

She spins round looking for the corridor down
which they came. It should be easy to spot for the lat-
ticed dome of sticks is now lit up in the jittery light
but she can see no opening. Has the wood collapsed,
blocking off her exit? Could such a thing happen
without her hearing or feeling it?

If she were a cat or a dog or a rabbit she might be able to squirm her way out but the gaps between the branches of which the structure is made are too small for a human being. She grabs a long pole in the least dense part of the pyre and starts to pull but as she does so she feels a great shifting in the spars above. She tries doing the same thing on the opposite side of the chamber but it has the same effect. She turns back to her father. His face is alight now, flesh spitting like meat on a barbecue, lips gone, teeth snapping in the heat. The wood above his head is ablaze and the flames are running like excited children outwards and upwards through all the airways in the great wooden maze.

'Carol . . . ?'

She can feel her hands and face blistering. She is going to die in here. Her father takes a couple of frail steps in her direction and lifts the oxygen mask towards her face. 'Breathe. Trust me. Just breathe.'

MARK HADDON grew up in Northampton. He read English at Merton College, Oxford and gained an Msc in Literature from the University of Edinburgh before making his foray into writing. His first book, *Gilbert's Gobstopper*, followed the adventures of a lost gobstopper and paved the way for many more children's books, including the *Agent-Z* series. Mark's debut novel, *The Curious Incident of the Dog in the Night-Time* won the 2003 Whitbread Award and has gone on to be one of the bestselling books of the last twenty years, with its play adaption winning seven Olivier awards.

Mark has since written three other novels – *A Spot of Bother*, *The Red House* and *The Porpoise* – and one short story collection, *The Pier Falls*.

A SPOT OF BOTHER

At fifty-seven, George is settling down to a comfortable retirement, building a shed in his garden, reading historical novels, listening to a bit of light jazz. Then Katie, his tempestuous daughter, announces that she is getting remarried, to Ray. Her family is not pleased – as her brother Jamie observes, Ray has 'strangler's hands'. Katie can't decide if she loves Ray, or loves the way he cares for her son Jacob, and her mother Jean is a bit put out by the way the wedding planning gets in the way of her affair with one of her husband's former colleagues. Meanwhile, the tidy and pleasant life Jamie has created crumbles when he fails to invite his lover, Tony, to the dreaded nuptials.

Unnoticed in the uproar, George discovers a sinister lesion on his hip, and quietly begins to lose his mind.

'A painful, funny, humane novel: beautifully written, addictively readable and so confident' *The Times*

'Wry, warm-hearted and entertaining' *Daily Telegraph*

THE RED HOUSE

Angela and her brother Richard have spent twenty years avoiding each other. Now, after the death of their mother, they bring their families together for a holiday in a rented house on the Welsh border. Four adults and four children. Seven days of shared meals, log fires, card games and wet walks.

But in the quiet and stillness of the valley, ghosts begin to rise up. The parents Richard thought he had. The parents Angela thought she had. Past and present lovers. Friends, enemies, victims, saviours.

'A hugely enjoyable, sympathetic novel . . . a tremendous pleasure . . . we have been absorbed, entertained and moved' *Observer*

'Shockingly well-observed, gut-wrenchingly familiar and even heartbreaking at times' *Stylist*

THE PIER FALLS

An expedition to Mars goes terribly wrong.
A seaside pier collapses.
A thirty-stone man is confined to his living room.
One woman is abandoned on a tiny island in the
middle of the ocean.
Another woman is saved from drowning.
Two boys discover a gun in a shoebox.
A group of explorers find a cave of unimaginable size
deep in the Amazon jungle.
A man shoots a stranger in the chest on Christmas Eve.

In this first collection of stories by the author of *The
Curious Incident of the Dog in the Night-Time* Mark Haddon
demonstrates two things: first that he is a master of the
short form; second that his imagination is even darker
than we had thought.

'A superb collection of stand-out stories . . . *The Pier Falls*
is unique in that every story is brilliant . . . It is, simply,
and ultimately, an absolute pleasure to read'
Irish Independent

'Outstanding . . . It feels as though Haddon is leading
you into the deepest underworld of human endeavour
and behaviour, yet holding your hand gently as he guides
you into the labyrinth' *Daily Mail*

THE PORPOISE

A newborn baby is the sole survivor of a terrifying plane crash.

She is raised in wealthy isolation by an overprotective father. She knows nothing of the rumours about a beautiful young woman, hidden from the world.

When a suitor visits, he understands far more than he should. Forced to run for his life, he escapes aboard *The Porpoise*, an assassin on his tail . . .

So begins a wild adventure of a novel, damp with salt spray, blood and tears. A novel that leaps from the modern era to ancient times; a novel that soars, and sails, and burns long and bright; a novel that almost drowns in grief yet swims ashore; in which pirates rampage, a princess wins a wrestler's hand, and ghost women with lampreys' teeth drag a man to hell – and in which the members of a shattered family, adrift in a violent world, journey towards a place called home.

'Mark Haddon cuts right down to the grittiness of humanity every time he writes. *The Porpoise* is a beautiful, unputdownable, ancient tangle with its own sweeping tides and dangerous depths' Daisy Johnson

VINTAGE MINIS

The Vintage Minis bring you the world's greatest writers on the experiences that make us human. These stylish, entertaining little books explore the whole spectrum of life – from birth to death, and everything in between. Which means there's something here for everyone, whatever your story.

vintageminis.co.uk